Dearest Daughter

Volume 2 of The Sisters' Saga

Alison Ferguson

Backstory Press

For Ian

Contents

Chapter 1

He sounds like a right charmer

The old house was too close to the flood-prone Parramatta River for peace of mind and too far from the track that wound through the Aylesford estate from the main road. Everyone said so, particularly the inhabitants of the farmhouse, the Burbridge family. Higher up the slope rose the skeleton of their new house, surrounded by stacks of lumber and blocks of sandstone scarred with convict chisels. In the still morning dark, the raw timbers assumed a false polish, wet with rain from earlier in the night.

A glint in an upstairs window flared, then shrank as the lantern-holder adjusted the screw. The light swayed, passed by the window, and reappeared downstairs. The hand that held the lantern was small, finely boned—a young woman's hand. Her figure was draped in woollen shawls, her stockinged feet thrust into sheepskin slippers. She moved about the ground floor of the house, every so often setting the lantern down to free her hands. In the hallway, she sorted the cards left by the visitors of the preceding day and arranged them in the silver salver reserved for that purpose. She did this several times until, content, she moved on.

Entering the kitchen, she paused, gazing down at the rough bundle of clothes curled among a nest of blankets by the cold hearth. She nudged the clothes with her toe.

A face, puffy with sleep, emerged and stared at her blearily. 'Yes, Miss Beth?'

'The fire, Susan.'

'Sorry, sorry, Miss Beth.'

They spoke quietly, the last ebb of night pressing down about them with the sanctity of a church.

The calm induced by her morning ritual wouldn't last. Already she could feel the bile rising from her empty stomach. She began to refold the pile of napkins that Susan had in readiness to be taken into the breakfast table. It would be all right. Henrietta's husband, Mr Richeley, would come and this time he'd get along with Papa and Mama. She shook out the cloth and started again. And then Henrietta and her children would leave with him and then everything would be back to the way it was. She ran her fingers along each crease, pressing so that it stayed flat. Rose would laugh again, and the two of them would get back to their collection—there were still so many flowers they had yet to sort and draw.

The door banged open and the rush of early morning air brought with it Jack, bearing a load of firewood from the shed. Behind him bustled Cook, or Mrs Holder as she preferred to be addressed, now that her sentence had been completed.

'And so what will it be for breakfast today, Miss Beth?' Mrs Holder began her preparations without waiting for a reply. She knew the movements of everyone in the household better than any of them and that included Beth, who was the only member of the family who took an interest in such details.

'Something light for the four of us heading into Sydney town to welcome Mr Richeley. We need to be off early.'

'And a tray for Mrs Richeley, I suppose,' interrupted Susan.

'That's enough of that tone from you, missie,' said Mrs Holder. 'And it's none of your beeswax anyway. That's Sarah's job.'

'If she can be bothered,' Susan muttered under her breath.

Beth was used to their bickering. They held their tongues in the presence of her mother, Mrs Burbridge, and were mindful around her sisters and brothers, but they barely registered her presence.

Beth cleared her throat. 'And dinner, of course, when we return with—'

'With Mr Richeley,' Mrs Holder cut in. 'Yes, all sorted, Miss Beth. Don't you be worrying about a thing. I've got a nice mulligatawny soup to start. Mr Richeley was partial to that last time he was here, I remember—said my soup was a good as any he'd had in India.'

'He sounds like a right charmer,' said Susan.

Susan is right about that, Beth thought. They'd all met Henrietta's husband once before, when he'd passed through Sydney on a trading voyage to South America. Back then she'd been still young enough to dream of buccaneers and adventures. For a long while afterwards, the pirate captain of her dreams looked very much like Mr Patrick Richeley.

'That'll be trouble,' grumbled Mrs Holder, cocking an ear to the sound of running footsteps. 'Them Richeley boys are a right bad influence if you ask me. Little Master Edward and Arthur were such good lads before they come 'ere to stay. Too used to being waited on hand and foot back in India, if you ask me.'

Mrs Holder's sentiments echoed those of Mr and Mrs Burbridge. The farmhouse had been too small for their own family's needs and, since the arrival of Henrietta and her children four years ago, the household had seethed with the ensuing friction.

Four heads poked around the door, expectant smiles held in check—Henrietta's sons Artie and Alec, and the Burbridge's youngest sons, Edward and Arthur.

'Please, Mrs Holder, please?'

Beth found it difficult not to smile as Mrs Holder made a show of lumbering over to the barrel of apples by the larder steps.

'There you go,' she said, deftly tossing each apple one after the next in their direction, grinning as they leapt and dived over each other to catch them. 'And don't be coming back until the grown-ups have eaten. And mind you stay out of the mud,' she called after them as they raced away.

Beth followed the boys out and found them sitting on the verandah steps, munching their apples. She sat with them, enjoying their unthinking contentment. A few swirls of mist lingered along the river below, disturbed by the first few rowboats setting out about the day's business.

'Are you looking forward to seeing your Papa this evening, Artie?' she asked the older of Henrietta's children.

Artie, tall for his years, shrugged, his mouth too full for speech.

His brother, Alec, spoke in his stead. 'Mama says I look exactly like him.'

The Burbridge boys broke into giggles.

'What?' Alec gave Edward a hard poke in the ribs.

'You don't even know what your father looks like,' Arthur jeered as he joined Edward in trying to tackle Alec.

Alec was the youngest but he could be slippery, and the wrestle ended up in an amicable truce. They fell to disputing which of them could spit their pips the furthest.

Beth rose to go, her equilibrium restored.

Artie followed her. 'Eliza has been crying,' he said quietly. 'Grandmama says she's not to go with Mama to the wharf to see Papa.' He spoke in a rush as though he thought he might get into trouble for telling her.

Beth nodded. She'd been there when the matter had been discussed. It had been closer to an argument than a discussion, in truth. Rose had insisted that she was only too happy to give up her place in the carriage for Eliza to go, but Mrs Burbridge was adamant that since there wasn't room for all the children, then none of them could go. 'No playing favourites,' she'd said. Henrietta had persevered, of course. Henrietta never recognised that the harder their parents were pressed, the more stubbornly they refused to budge. The altercation had reached the point where their mother had declared that their father would be the only one to go, before Henrietta relented.

'Never mind,' Beth patted Artie on the shoulder. 'You'll all see him this evening.'

She could hear the sounds of the household starting to stir. If she could rout out Sarah from wherever she was lazing and get Henrietta's breakfast tray on its way to her, then perhaps the day could start smoothly.

Chapter 2

I see the situation all too clearly

Beth held her handkerchief up to her nose. The cologne she'd dabbed on it earlier couldn't mask the stench of the Sydney quayside. From inside the carriage, she watched her father's top hat as he wended his way imperiously through the crowds on the wharf. Mr Burbridge wasn't a tall man—of average height and increasingly inclined to stockiness as he was ageing—but he behaved as if he were. His demeanour, along with the top hat, gave the impression of bulk and a certain grandeur of presence. Accordingly, the crowd parted before him.

Reaching their carriage, he barked, 'Delayed, of course. Some fool of a captain jumped in on the *Mary Hope*'s mooring rights at first light. Campbell swears he can't do anything about it until they've finished getting the stock off.' He spoke loudly to the air in general, as was his wont.

In this instance, it was Henrietta who took it upon herself to respond. 'No doubt my husband will make his way over to us in his own good time. I'm sure he has matters to attend to.' She spoke through gritted teeth.

'Is four years not long enough for the man to complete his business?' said Mr Burbridge with asperity. He stood, feet planted apart, his hands on his hips, surveying the scene before him. 'Ah, good, Mr Avery has his skiff over there. Griffith, go and see if he'll go out to the *Mary Hope* and take Richeley off.'

At his father's words, Griffith, who stood propped against the side of the carriage, opened his eyes, wincing in pain at the glare of sunlight. He'd spent the night before in town and had led his horse down to the wharf, too fragile to mount. If he'd slept at all, it had been in his clothes. He looked blearily in the direction his father was indicating.

Mr Burbridge gave him a sour look. 'Time you made yourself useful for once. Get down there and see what you can organise.'

Henrietta sighed and slid over to where the sun shafted through the open door of the carriage. Beside her, Rose shivered in the fresh breeze coming off the harbour.

'Are you cold, Rose? Would you like my shawl?' Beth asked.

'Cold?' Mr Burbridge spoke in the general direction of the harbour. 'It's not cold. Nothing like back home.'

Beth knew her father meant England. To the older Burbridge children—Henrietta, Bill, Griffith and Rose—England was 'home' because they'd been born there and spent their early childhood on the family estate in Kent. Beth was the only one in the family who didn't call England home. She had been born in the colony a few months after their arrival. Perhaps it was because she'd been named after their new country—Beth Australia Burbridge. She loved her name. It was one of the few things she did like about herself.

'But the August breeze is chilly, Papa. Spring isn't quite with us.' Beth held out her shawl to her sister.

Rose took it without acknowledgement. Her fit of pique had lasted from last night's argument right through the fifteen-mile journey into Sydney town from Parramatta.

'What's he up to?' Mr Burbridge said, looking about. 'You'd think a man who's spent his life around boats could rustle up ...' His voice died away as Griffith approached.

'Avery couldn't manage it, but Lieutenant McAllister was more than happy to oblige. He's down to sail his boat out to welcome the Bougainville lot—wants to give his crew a quick shakedown run. Doesn't want to embarrass himself in front of the Frenchies. He'll be out and back from the *Mary Hope* before you know it.'

Mr Burbridge gave a grunt of acknowledgement and continued his pacing.

Campbells Wharf was seething with people, carts and drays in the everyday bedlam that marked the unloading of vessels. The ships tied up by the wharf were moored abreast so that the men ran from one deck to another across a network of planks bringing the goods from the outer ships to land.

Griffith poked his head into the carriage. His breath was rank with stale tobacco and spirits and some other sweet smell that Beth couldn't recognise. She put her handkerchief to her nose again.

'Pity your children couldn't come,' he said to Henrietta. 'Richeley's sure to be expecting to see them. Artie and Alec would have loved a chance to get this close to the ships.'

'Well, you know Mother,' Henrietta said tersely.

'It can hardly matter to your children, surely,' Rose interjected. 'They won't recognise their father after four years. Artie and Alec weren't even five when you arrived back from Calcutta.'

Henrietta's eyes narrowed. 'Much the same age as you and Beth when Papa returned from England after four years away. You remember, Griffith? They were terrified of him for weeks. Beth didn't speak for almost three months whenever he was in the room.'

The words stung, although Beth had heard the tale many times before.

Henrietta added, so quietly that Beth had to strain to make out the words, 'All the same, I would have liked little Eliza to come. Richeley does so dote on her. Such a pretty girl.' She absentmindedly patted a loose curl into place with a gloved hand.

Mr Burbridge lifted an arm in a stately wave as several frock-coated gentlemen approached. The noise of the wharf prevented Beth hearing what they were saying, but the topic evidently concerned shipping by the way they all looked out across the harbour.

Griffith followed her gaze. 'They'll be telling Father about de Bougainville's ships.'

'De Bougainville, you say?' said Henrietta. 'The explorer? I thought he was dead. Or should be, by now.'

'Not that de Bougainville.' Griffith smiled. 'It's his son—Baron Hyacinthe de Bougainville. I heard all about it last night. Their ships have already been sighted off Botany Bay. They're doing the full circumnavigation.' Griffith's apparent malaise from the previous evening dissolved as he discussed the sailing exploits of the French expedition. 'And there he is.'

For an absurd moment, Beth thought he meant de Bougainville but, as her father's head swung in the direction of a cluster of passengers being helped up to the wharf, she realised that Griffith was talking about Mr Richeley.

The tallest of the gentlemen disengaged from the group and, after pausing to give orders as to the disposition of his luggage, he made his way through the crowds. He was not at all as Beth remembered. He looked older than his thirty years, his gait slowed by the weight he carried about his belly. As he drew closer, she saw that his face and nose were ruddy, his jawline obscured by fleshy jowls.

Henrietta sat rigidly still beside her until Richeley had greeted Mr Burbridge. Only as he turned towards the carriage did Henrietta move forward and descend gracefully to the ground.

'Mrs Richeley.' Something like awe crossed Richeley's face as he looked at his wife.

Beth knew that expression well. It was the way every gentleman of their acquaintance looked on greeting Henrietta. Feature by feature, Henrietta was not a beauty. She wasn't pretty like Rose, nor handsome like their mother. However, her features taken all together, combined with her teasing eyes and wit, meant that if she chose, she captured and played with male attention like a cat. Perhaps, in the four years they had been apart, he'd forgotten her magic.

'Mr Richeley.' Henrietta inclined her head ever so slightly.

Then Richeley moved forward, as if to embrace her, but Henrietta forestalled him. She stretched out an arm, her gloved hand proffered in readiness for his salutation.

Richeley grazed the silken fabric with his lips. 'It's been too long,' he said.

'Indeed it has,' Henrietta retorted.

Griffith cleared his throat as he obviously worked to find something to fill the silence. 'Oh, look, see there—the French expedition rounding the point, if I'm not mistaken.'

In silence, they watched as the boats sailed closer. As the cannon on Dawes Point sounded its welcome, the French sailors and their officers lining the deck stood to attention.

'The frigate is *Thétis* and the corvette is *L'Ésperance.'* Griffith pointed each of them out.

'Good-looking boats,' Henrietta said. 'And all hands on deck, by the look of them. French sailors have a certain something about them—it must be their uniforms.'

Richeley scowled.

'I do hope Rose will have a chance to be introduced to the commodore,' Henrietta added sweetly.

After the tedious wait for Richeley's luggage to be strapped to the roof of the carriage, Mr Burbridge kept them a further hour while he disappeared into one of the nearby warehouses.

'I thought Father wanted to get back to Aylesford as soon as he could,' Rose said petulantly.

'He certainly made a big enough fuss about having to come into town,' Henrietta agreed.

'It's the building of the new house,' Griffith explained to Richeley. 'He has to check every detail.'

'Leave the experts to it, that's my motto,' said Richeley. 'The more ideas you contribute, the more it's going to cost you. Why, our bungalow back in Agra cost—'

Henrietta cut him off with a meaningful look. 'I daresay he'll be currying favour with Mr McPhail and his cronies.'

When Mr Burbridge finally emerged, he called up to the coachman, 'This is going to take longer than I'd anticipated, Chapman. No need to wait. And Richeley, I'll have the pleasure of talking with you when I get back to Aylesford.' The way he said it sounded like a threat.

At being thus addressed, Richeley nodded curtly and began to climb into the carriage.

'Do you want me to stay?' Griffith asked his father. 'If it's about the seal skins—?'

'Nothing to do with you. You go with your sisters.'

Griffith's face was set as he turned to unhitch the reins of his horse. However, his tone was light enough as he called after Richeley, 'I can get you a horse, Richeley, old man. I bet you'd like a ride after being cooped up at sea for so long.'

'No need to trouble yourself. Nothing I enjoy more than being surrounded by such examples of feminine beauty.' He accompanied the laboured compliment with a bow of the head.

'Well, if you're sure ...?' Griffith looked to Henrietta.

She gave a barely perceptible shrug.

Getting out of Sydney town was slow going. The heavy rains of the night before meant that the top layer of dirt had turned to muddy slush. With each jarring pothole, sticky ochre splattered the carriage wheels and sides. With the canvas blinds fastened, the carriage was stuffy. Richeley made to roll up the blind beside him.

'Leave it down,' Henrietta said. 'I may be wearing spotted muslin, but I have no wish for any more spots.' She flicked her hands along the fabric as though brushing off a newly arrived offender.

Richeley left the blind alone and leaned back, surveying her coolly. 'It's a lovely dress, to be sure. So who paid for it, might I ask? Your father or myself?'

Henrietta ignored him.

Beth saw Rose's lips twitch. The fabric Henrietta had bought for the dress was the rich yellow of the honey that they drew from their hives, worked with ink-black embroidery. The whole household had heard the uproar that had resulted from her purchase. Every word of their father's reproach and their mother's scolding had resonated through the small farmhouse.

To Beth's relief, marital hostilities were interrupted when they reached the tollgates on the outskirts of the town.

'A spot of trouble ahead, sir,' Chapman called to Griffith, who was riding alongside.

Soon after the carriage stopped, Griffith came back to let them know what was going on. 'Might as well get out and stretch your legs a bit,' he said. 'They've managed to catch a couple of absconders hiding in one of the carts up ahead. We'll be here until they've sorted it out.'

Only Rose remained in the carriage, her gloved finger tracing down the margin of each densely printed page of her book before moving on to the next. The surrounding bush was alive with the shrieks and screams of feuding birds. The sun was high in the sky, and Beth tipped her head back and closed her eyes, relishing the spring warmth. *In a few days, I'll need to carry my parasol.*

'I'd forgotten all of this when I returned four years ago.' Henrietta indicated the bright blue sky to Richeley. 'The heat in India bakes and broils you, but here, it bites. Are bonnets back in fashion in Calcutta now?' She didn't wait for an answer. 'You know, no one was wearing bonnets there when I left. I had to buy one especially when my ship stopped off in Hobart. Goodness knows what Mama would have said if I had arrived in Sydney bonnetless. Better I arrived entirely headless than that.'

This was another tale Beth had heard before, but Henrietta included her in her audience as she kept up her stream of relentless chat.

Beth searched for some reply. She wanted to say something witty, something that would let Henrietta know that she understood her chatter was a barrier to repel any further attacks from Richeley. But wit was not in her armoury; she had nothing to offer.

However, Henrietta continued seamlessly. 'And this road was much changed as well. Bridges everywhere. When did you say they built all these bridges, Griffith?'

'I'm sure at least some of them were here when you left,' he said, preoccupied with checking the bridle on his horse.

'I remember when there were none at all—and we had five creeks to ford to get to Aylesford. Do you remember that first trip, Griffith? In the gig with Papa?'

From behind her, Beth heard Rose's irritated sigh coming from the carriage.

'I wasn't in the gig, remember,' Griffith answered, now agreeably playing his part in the story. 'You were the one who got to go with Papa. I was stuck with Rose in the carriage with Mama.' He affected a mock-childish pout. 'And Bill rode with Mr Ridgeway on the bullock wagon—later he kept on about how he got to use the whip.' Even as he joked, a note of bitterness still tinged the recollection.

'And there you have it, Griffith,' said Henrietta. 'The reason in a nutshell why you ended up so good with the ladies and Bill ended up so good with—' She broke off as Griffith guffawed.

Richeley, who had been following the conversation, forced a polite smile.

Beth couldn't feign amusement. None of these were her memories. She felt oddly defensive of her brother Bill. Normally she thought of him as a boorish oaf, more at home with his stock from the Burbridge properties up in the Hunter. Now she wanted to snap that at least their brother wasn't the sort of person to collapse into immature giggling at the slightest thing.

The rest of the journey proceeded in silence until the carriage left Parramatta Road and turned onto the track that led through the Aylesford estate.

With the house in sight, Richeley regrouped. 'I'm looking forward to seeing Eliza. I had hoped she might be included in the welcoming party. I hope she is well?'

'And your sons?' Henrietta asked. 'Artie and Alec—'

'Artie?'

'You do remember your eldest son, Arthur, I presume?'

Richeley glowered. 'Not as Artie.'

Beth's back ached as she tensed for the impending argument. But Henrietta and her husband held their fire—circling each other, as combatants do: probing, needling, seeking advantageous footing.

'Two young boys with the same name, you see,' Beth blurted, no longer able to stand the silence. 'Our

brother Arthur is a few years older than your Arthur,
so—'

'Yes, I do see,' Richeley snapped, never taking his
eyes off Henrietta. 'I see the situation all too clearly.'

Chapter 3

A dearth of quality gentlemen

Beth watched Henrietta as she trailed her fingers through the cool water over the side of the rowboat. Eliza dangled her hand alongside her mother's. At nine, she was still affectionate and impulsive with her hugs. Beth envied Henrietta the feel of a child's arm crooked around her neck. Griffith had the oars and began to pull back towards the shore. Henrietta's sons sat on either side of him, their hands gripped around the oars, sure that they were the ones in charge; Artie hauling valiantly and Alec getting in the way.

'Is that one of the French officers with Rose and Mama?' Henrietta asked, indicating the bank where the picnickers had laid their rugs and baskets.

'It's the commodore himself—Baron de Bougainville. Met him with Father when we were at the Buff's Regimental dinner the other night.' Griffith puffed with the exertion of pulling against the current of the Parramatta River. 'You know Father, never one for holding back when talking to someone of importance. He invited the chap to join us, even though it was only going to be a family-do.' He drew a rasping breath. 'And then he and Bill headed into the scrub with the dogs to see what they could shoot, and so they aren't here to welcome him.'

'You're out of condition, Griffith. I don't care what you say, smoking that much opium can't be good for you.'

'Nonsense. Fumigates the lungs—everyone in Canton smokes. If it's not cholera, then it's the plague—you've got to smoke.'

'De Bougainville,' mused Henrietta. 'He looks to be younger than I expected.'

'Get lively with that rudder, Beth,' Griffith instructed as he began to row the little boat cross-current to get back into shore.

Once there, Artie and Alec leapt out and ran about the shoreline getting their feet wet and muddy. Beth followed the others as they walked towards the picnickers: the younger adults and children sprawled on cushions, the older members ensconced on chairs brought along by the servants. Baron de Bougainville looked to be in his forties, she calculated, although there was not a trace of grey in his thick dark hair. Rose was practising her French with him, and their mother was encouraging her. Henrietta's husband had decamped within minutes of arrival at the picnic, promising not to be absent long but, by the look of it, he was still not back.

The baron rose to his feet as they approached. Henrietta headed to a spare cushion by his side, but her mother had other ideas.

'Come and sit beside me, Henrietta dear. Leave some room for Baron de Bougainville.' She turned briefly to the baron. 'May I introduce my eldest daughter, Mrs Richeley. Oh, and Beth, of course,' she added as an afterthought.

'I am enchanted to make your acquaintance, Madame Richeley, Mademoiselle.' He bowed to each of them more deeply than was usual in the colony.

Eliza fell into shy giggles.

Once they had been settled, de Bougainville resumed his seat and continued his previous conversation with Rose, but now in lightly accented English. 'Yes, I was here as a young man with the Baudin expedition.' He smiled, clearly reminiscing. 'And I stayed a little longer than my ship, I'm afraid.'

He left the sentence hanging, tantalising. Beth longed to hear more. She knew Rose was far too well bred to ask. But there was something dangerous in his eyes, something that dared his listeners to question him further. Perhaps Henrietta would enquire. But she stayed silent—as if refusing to be drawn in.

It was little Eliza who asked the question. 'But if your ship left without you, how did you get home?'

Henrietta gave her a fond pat on the head.

De Bougainville's smile broadened. 'It seems to me that the English have created this prison so far from civilisation as a mere pretext for hiding their most beautiful ladies from the rest of the world. Or perhaps it is just your family, Madame Burbridge? I see before me three of the loveliest young women in existence.'

'Four,' blurted Eliza, immediately looking overwhelmed by her temerity.

De Bougainville gave the hint of a wink. '*Mais, bien sûr, mademoiselle*, one more waiting in the wings.'

Eliza collapsed into giggles again.

'In fact, I am amazed that only one has been claimed in a colony so overly-populated with men,' he continued. Perhaps it was the pang that passed over Mrs Burbridge's countenance that prompted him to add, 'Though, of course, I am immensely grateful for what must be a dearth of quality in the gentlemen of New South Wales.'

As he continued talking with her sisters, Beth was content to accept the signals from her mother to leave the conversational stage free for Rose. She barely listened, though she supposed he must be amusing, given Rose's lively responses. It was always hard to predict how Rose would react in any social encounter where gentlemen were present. Sometimes, she would sparkle and smile and be entirely captivating. At other times, she would declare the company to be insufferably dull and not worth the time away from her consuming interest with all things botanical.

But de Bougainville had drawn forth the most interest that Beth had ever seen her sister display. She could see the attraction. His legs, long and clad in Navy whites, stretched across the picnic blanket. Even in his forties, no chairs for him. She glanced to the chair they'd left empty for when Richeley returned. As the baron talked with Rose, he kept looking in Henrietta's direction. Perhaps, she was mistaken. Henrietta was sitting next to her mother, after all. Perhaps he was regarding them both.

'Ah, Mr Richeley has decided to join us,' Mrs Burbridge said.

Turning, Beth could see him riding along the short track from the roadway. He should have left the horse there, she thought, where Mr Chapman could have helped him dismount. Henrietta had told her that she and Mr Richeley used to own two of the finest greys in Calcutta. But he didn't sit a horse well. The extra weight that had built around his girth didn't keep him in the saddle any better now as he bounced out of rhythm with his mount.

When he reached them, he looked about for a servant.

Griffith, spotting his dilemma, went over and discretely assisted him to reach the ground. 'Let's show the boys how it's done.' Griffith gestured to where a rough game of cricket was in progress. 'Time that someone other than Edward got to bat,' he called to where Artie and Alec were playing with the youngest Burbridge sons, Edward and Arthur. Edward, claiming the rights of the eldest, had been batting for most of the picnic.

The novelty of having their father join them excited Artie and Alec into a complete inability to focus on the game. They hopped from one foot to the other, shrieking encouragement and howling with despair when he failed to get more than two runs off a ball unanimously declared to be a six, given it was lost to sight in the scrub.

Red-faced and out-of-breath, both Griffith and Richeley left it to the boys to search for it. Griffith sank to the cushions. Richeley lowered himself into the chair.

After introductions had been made, de Bougainville asked, 'I understand that you are soon to return to Calcutta, Monsieur Richeley?'

'Mrs Richeley and I hope to be gone before summer is upon us. Business is keeping me here a little longer than I'd hoped. I'm looking into some property that Mr Campbell, my agent, has recommended.'

'Such is the lot of businessmen like yourself— always needing to be on the lookout for new investments. We simple sailors merely hope for favourable tides and fair winds.'

'As someone with a foot in both camps, I can assure you that finance is as fickle as the weather,' Griffith said. 'I keep swearing that each voyage for Dent and Company will be my last, but with trade the way it is, I can't for the life of me see how I can afford it.'

De Bougainville looked to Henrietta. 'I imagine your children must be looking forward to going home.'

'They'll be staying here,' Richeley answered for her.

Startled, Henrietta stared at her husband, biting off a sharp contradiction.

'They are not to travel with you?'

The baron had directed his question to Henrietta, but again it was Richeley who replied.

'I have been confirming arrangements this very morning. At Mrs Burbridge's kind suggestion.' He nodded in acknowledgement in the direction of his mother-in-law. 'I have arranged for Reverend and Mrs Wilkinson to look to them and their education.' He didn't look at Henrietta.

De Bougainville continued to look puzzled. Beth could almost anticipate his next question, for it was the question in her own mind—were the children to live with the Wilkinsons?

'Should we be packing up, do you think?' Mrs Burbridge signalled to the servants. 'If we leave it much later, the mosquitos will be picnicking on us.' As she spoke, Mr Burbridge and Bill returned, guns under their arms, but otherwise empty-handed.

De Bougainville rose to his feet, grace in every movement, and the men exchanged greetings.

'Sorry you couldn't join us,' said Mr Burbridge. 'But you didn't miss any sport. It looks like those fires the damn blacks were setting through here have moved the game on.'

'You let them onto your property? I thought most of the local tribes had moved inland — or, at least, that's what I heard. We have seen so few, and they are an unprepossessing lot.'

'Just because you don't see them, doesn't mean they're not here.' Mr Burbridge scanned the bush. 'Eyes everywhere, if you ask me. But generally, they keep out of the way, down here at least. They know what's good for them. Much more of a problem on our property up north. Bill can tell you.'

However, Bill wasn't attending to the conversation. His eyes followed the servants who had begun to pack up the picnic things. Susan was balancing large piles of cushions, and Mary was collecting the chairs.

Her brother's focus on the servants was so unusual that Beth was puzzled. Then she saw that Sarah, who gloried in referring to herself as Henrietta's lady's maid, was coming back up the bank from where she'd been assiduously staying out of work's way. She was their latest girl from the Female Orphan School and, although her face was plain, her figure was full and comely.

As the party began to amble back along the track, Beth was behind Henrietta when de Bougainville moved beside her sister. Henrietta darted a look about her, perhaps checking for her husband. He was still, rather ineffectually, trying to round up the boys ready for leaving.

De Bougainville spoke in a low voice. 'Your children, they will not stay with your own family?'

Beth saw Henrietta's head drop.

De Bougainville's hand touched the small of Henrietta's back as he moved to support her when she stumbled on the rough ground.

And the acacias were looking wonderful

'The wattle is more profuse here, don't you think, Rose?' Beth essayed conversation to relieve the boredom.

'Yes, I daresay it is,' Rose replied with a shrug.

Rose was brooding again. Judging by the dark looks she headed in Henrietta's direction, it was clear where her thoughts lay. Her mood since meeting de Bougainville had been unpredictable. At times, she was interested in all her usual pursuits and she continued to be charming if they had company. However, Henrietta kept teasing her about the baron and, the more Rose reacted, the more Henrietta delighted in the sport.

Beth tried resting her elbow on the carriage window ledge to gain some stability as the carriage jolted along the track. The trip to Emu Plains was long and tedious, and the afternoon squall that had blown through had added to the humidity. The track had become rougher as they moved beyond the more settled areas around Parramatta, and Mr Chapman's frequent refreshment from his flask of brandy meant that he wasn't as judicious in his driving as she would have preferred.

In the absence of further conversation, Beth fell back into her own worries. She couldn't shake what her mother had said before they left.

'Beth, a moment.' Mrs Burbridge had beckoned her back out of the entrance hall where they waited for the carriage to be brought around.

She'd searched her conscience. Her mother only ever spoke to her alone if she had failed in her duties, and Beth did her best to avoid this. Occasionally, her mother would declare to some visitor or other that 'Beth is a good girl', but she never said such things to her face. Beth didn't know whether her mother was being sincere about what she said to the visitors or about what she omitted to say in their absence.

'Henrietta is insisting that she will go to the performance with you all, without waiting for Richeley to get back from his business in town,' Mrs Burbridge said, pacing. 'Why the man couldn't make the effort to come back last night, I don't know. I would come along if I could get away, but I promised Mrs Wood that I'd call—she's so poorly, I don't want to let her down. You'll need to be on your guard.'

Relief mingled with disappointment. This was not about her. She struggled to catch her mother's meaning. Finally, it came to her. 'Is Baron de Bougainville to be there?'

Mrs Burbridge smiled thinly. 'Yes, yes, that's it. That's it exactly. You know what Henrietta can be like.

And it's not fair on Rose.' She patted Beth's hand. 'I'm sure you'll do just fine.'

She wasn't at all sure she would be able to do what her mother had asked. How could she keep Henrietta from flirting with de Bougainville? It was asking a bee to stay away from pollen—or was it de Bougainville who was the bee? She needed to stop thinking about it. 'Do we know what plays they'll be putting on?' she asked.

'Given the audience and the players, a comedy, I should think,' said Henrietta, 'though perhaps not suitable for young unmarried ladies.'

'Sir John wouldn't have suggested our attending otherwise,' Mr Burbridge said.

It was a relief to alight at Regentsville, Sir John Jamison's villa. Beth knew the house well, since Sir John loved to entertain. It stood two storeys high, situated on a rise. As they walked past the colonnade, which stretched along the verandah to their left and right, she saw her father touch one of the columns, as if in homage. This house was the model to which their own half-finished villa aspired. Her father had made endless plans and held discussions with every architect available, but raising the funds fought for priority with the demands of the estate.

No such restrictions appeared to have affected Sir John. The grand entrance hall was flanked by two large drawing rooms, a dining room, breakfast room, a study and a library. The circular staircase at the far end was made of stone. The Burbridge's fractiousness dissipated in the presence of such luxury.

Sir John's housekeeper, Mrs Griffiths, greeted them and organised for the servants to supply them with refreshments. She was a kind-faced woman and her figure had grown plump with successive children who, in the absence of a Mr Griffiths, were all reputed to be Sir John's.

'Sir John is already at the theatre,' she explained as she ushered them into the drawing room. 'He wanted a word with Mr Kinghorne, the superintendent, before it starts. But the McPhails will be here any minute, I expect, so you'll all be able to head over to the river together in the punt.'

The McPhails were indeed close behind them. Mr and Mrs McPhail were frequent visitors, so the chat was familiar and relaxed. Beth sipped her tea and watched.

'Have you heard about the latest debacle?' asked Mr McPhail, addressing himself to Mr Burbridge. 'Governor Brisbane has made another botch of things. Thinks he can override the Assignment Board and claw back our assigned convicts for the use of the Australian Agricultural Company. The Colonial Office is trying to have it both ways—they think they can grant our allocation and then change their mind whenever suits. We could be doing with another governor, if you ask me.'

'It doesn't matter who the Colonial Office appoints,' said Mr Burbridge. 'At the end of the day, we have a military government, and the rights of free settlers such as ourselves are the least of their priorities.'

'Why, man,' said Mr McPhail, 'you sound as if you're ready to pack it in.'

'Not at all.' Mr Blaxand looked grim.

Mrs McPhail and Henrietta were deep in quiet conversation. The two women were about the same age and shared a love of fashion and gossip. They sat side by side on the sofa, leaving Rose marooned from the conversation.

'So, Mr Richeley isn't with you? I thought you two wouldn't be letting each other out of sight after such a long time apart.' Mrs McPhail gave a roguish smile.

'You've been married for how long?' Henrietta enquired.

'Four years,' Mrs McPhail protested.

'Well, when you've been married eight years, I can assure you that absence and fondness are not inevitably associated with one another.'

'So how is your little Margaret, Mrs McPhail?' Rose asked.

'Perfectly well, Miss Burbridge. Margarette,' she said, stressing her preferred pronunciation of her daughter's name, 'is at home with her nurse for the evening.' She turned back to Henrietta. 'It's lovely to be going out to the theatre, even if it is a production from the Convict Farm. Who else is coming, do you know?'

'I think the Coxes are coming, and I did hear something about them bringing the Hawkins girls.'

'They're a bit young, aren't they?' interrupted Rose. 'Miss Hawkins is just out, and her sister is not even as old as Beth.'

Mrs McPhail looked cross. 'Sir John said that Mr Kinghorne assured him that the plays would be entirely respectable.'

'And we did hear that some of the French officers will be there,' said Henrietta, continuing her list of likely audience members.

'Oh.' Mrs McPhail gave a girlish giggle. 'Have you met Baron de Bougainville? I did hear that he is quite the handsomest gentleman.'

'I'm sure Rose considers him so,' said Henrietta.

Rose tapped the arm of her chair three times with her forefinger as a soldier counts down before firing.

Beth braced herself for the riposte.

'Time we were off,' called Mrs McPhail, clearly oblivious to the tension that had fallen between the sisters. 'Don't want to miss the opening act, do we?'

As the punt drew across the wide, slow waters of the Nepean, the sky was darkening. Along the banks, the Aboriginals had lit fires, luring the fish to the surface to their waiting spears.

Beth sat with her father and sisters among the *sterling*, as the convicts liked to call them. Their seats were in a roped-off section reserved for those in the top tier of the little society. The *currency*, those born in the colony, lounged about with a mix of other free settlers and emancipists. She knew many of them by sight, particularly those who ran local businesses.

The uniformed soldiers mingled with the currency, while their officers spent their time with the sterling. Outnumbering all of these by far were those still serving out their sentences. Having finished their assigned work for the day, they were free to earn some pennies as best they could or tend their gardens to supplement the government rations or, as they were doing now, to find what enjoyment they could. Usually, entertainment involved the consumption of rough locally made rum, this being a general term for anything resembling spirits. This occupation was shared across all levels of the colony; however, the quality of alcohol increased, according to rank. Tonight, this had the effect of adding to the enthusiasm with which the audience awaited the performance.

The back of her neck prickled. The French officers were seated behind where she sat with her sisters. Rose had coloured as de Bougainville bowed in greeting. He was accompanied by his second-in-command, Mr

Ducamper, the captain of the second vessel, *L'Ésperance,* who without de Bougainville by his side would have been called handsome. She listened to their murmurs and, despite her poor French, could make out they were struck by the idiosyncratic stage before them. It looked as though the carpenters had been more familiar with the construction of gallows. A rough curtain hung at the back of the raised platform and it rippled with the movements of those waiting for their moment on the stage.

The Lying Valet was the first item on the program. Beth was familiar with the play by Garrick and relaxed as she enjoyed the farce played out by four male convicts, two of them made up as the female characters—Melissa and her servant Kitty—much to the delight of the audience. The schemes and subterfuges of Sharp, the wily servant, as he tried to hide his master's impecunious state to his intended, Melissa, were as delightfully predictable as ever.

Sharp, played by an actor with an expressive face, flashed the audience a wicked grin as he addressed his master, Gayless. 'I have one scheme left which in all probability may succeed. The good citizen, overloaded with his last meal, is taking a nap in that closet, in order to get him an appetite for yours. Suppose, sir, we should make him treat us.'

Gayless was played by an Irishman who affected a tortured accent to display the noble rank of his character. He replied, 'I don't understand you.'

'I'll pick his pocket and provide us a supper with the booty.'

'Monstrous!' Gayless replied. Then, with a wink to the crowd, added, 'For without considering the villainy of it, the danger of waking him makes it impracticable!'

The audience jeered, 'Give it a shot, you pigeon-livered sod.'

Sharp waited until the catcalling died down, waggled his eyebrows and said, 'If he wakes, I'll smother him and lay his death to indigestion—a very common death among the Justices.'

There were roars of laughter at this, though not from the gentlemen who enjoyed their status as Magistrates and Justices of the Peace in the colony. It took some time before the play could proceed to its improbably happy conclusion.

There was a short break in proceedings as the rickety theatre was adjusted for the next item. Mrs Cox leaned over from her seat to talk with Mrs McPhail and Henrietta. Beth was relieved to see this, as it meant that when de Bougainville made his way around the seating, it was Rose who was first to gain his attention.

'Are you enjoying the play, Miss Burbridge?' de Bougainville enquired.

'Indeed.' Rose seemed to be at a loss for a reply. She gabbled, 'The trip out here was less enjoyable. I hope you weren't caught in the storm.'

Beth found she wasn't breathing. It was agonising to hear her sister, normally self-assured, so ill at ease.

'We were, but it was all part of the adventure.' De Bougainville's eyes had begun to wander over Rose's shoulder to where Henrietta was talking gaily with Mrs Cox.

Beth willed Henrietta to remain unaware of the baron's gaze.

'And the acacias were looking wonderful,' Rose sallied. Then, in a rush, she added, 'There are fifty-eight species of acacia, you know. Most people see the yellow bloom and call them wattle, but—'

'That is most fascinating.' The baron did not look the least interested. 'Perhaps we should take our seats. I think the performance is about to resume.'

The next piece was another play with which Beth was familiar: *The Village Doctor*. She had read it as part of her French lessons as Molière's *Le Médecin malgré lui*. She wondered if Mr Kinghorne had chosen it by way of a compliment to their French guests. The audience was less appreciative of this item. However, when a one-eyed man played what looked to be a homemade fiddle to accompany a dancing interlude, the crowd clapped along, with some eager souls leaping to their feet to link arms and twirl about.

The next intermission was long enough for refreshments to be served to the gentry.

Mr Kinghorne, a grave long-faced man, oversaw the convict servants assigned to the task while Sir John moved about, making sure he spoke to each of his guests.

Sir John carried himself with air of an English country squire. He was heavily built and had reached the stage of life and expanse of belly where the sticking of one's thumbs into the pockets of one's waistcoat presented the most comfortable way to stand and talk. 'Well done, by Jove,' he said in his fruity voice. 'Worth the price of admission, eh?'

They tittered at his little joke. The charge had been a mere fifteen pence, or a *dump*, as it was known. For Sir John, the total price for all of the guests was barely the cost of a bottle of imported wine. For the rest of the audience, they'd forgone a far greater proportion of their funds to attend.

In the cluster of people around Sir John, Beth had lost sight of Henrietta. It was Rose's expression that alerted her to trouble. Rose was staring, her expression fixed and baleful, to where Henrietta stood with de Bougainville. His back was towards them, so Beth couldn't see his face. But she could see Henrietta's: alight, glowing.

Mr Burbridge may have been also put on notice by his wife, as he moved to join the couple. He was courteous—de Bougainville was nobility after all—but it was with a firm hand that he took Henrietta's arm and ushered her back to her seat.

Perhaps the players had also indulged in some refreshment during the break, or possibly their aspiration to perform three plays in a single evening was overly ambitious, for the plot of the third item, *Bombastes Furioso*, was barely comprehensible. The parts of the plot Beth did grasp did nothing to ease her mind, however. The comic play was a new one, and she'd read about its performances in the excerpts from the London papers. The actor who'd appeared as the lying valet earlier in the evening, played the role of the King of Utopia, who was intent on divorcing his wife to marry Distaffina, despite her being betrothed to General Bombastes.

As the King leered and pressed half a crown on Distaffina to persuade her to abandon the General, Beth heard a quick in-breath from behind her. She longed to turn her head to see if it was de Bougainville who was so affected. Beside her, she saw Henrietta bow her head, her eyes upon her fingers as they worked to smooth her skirts. When Distaffina agreed, Henrietta's head flew up, her chin forward, almost defiant.

The General, played by the Irishman who'd appeared in the earlier play, made use of his adopted accent again for the role. On hearing of Distaffina's rejection, he ran about the stage in a torment usually displayed by headless chickens. In his madness, the General threw his boots over the branch of a tree. The prop used for the tree, under cover of bushy camouflage, looked to be the type of triangular frame used in the colony for meting out lashes. The General stuck a large sign on the purported tree and helpfully read it aloud for the illiterate majority of the audience.

'Who dares this pair of boots displace,

Must meet Bombastes face to face.'

At this, the audience, more in touch with the plot than Beth, yelled, 'A duel, a duel.'

Accordingly, the King cut down the boots and then, as promised, was killed by the General. Another character, Fusbos, whose role had been unclear throughout but who might have been the Prime Minister of Utopia, emerged and shot the General, who died in a slow dramatic fashion.

Turning to Distaffina, Fusbos sent her away, saying, 'Go, beauty, go, thou source of woe to man, and get another lover if you can.'

Then, the King and the General both leapt to their feet and swore to the audience, 'If some folks please, we'll die again tomorrow.'

With that, the company took their bows amid great applause.

Sir John's guests agreed that, all in all, it had been a wonderful entertainment. Mr Kinghorne was congratulated on his reforming efforts. Rose held her head averted from Beth's questioning gaze. Henrietta, on the other hand, was humming a tune under her breath.

Mr Burbridge shook de Bougainville's hand.

'Till we meet again, monsieur,' de Bougainville said. 'I look forward to it.'

Mr Burbridge, obviously caught off guard, covered his confusion. 'As do I, sir, as do I.'

As de Bougainville moved away, Mr Burbridge said, 'And when are we to have the pleasure of French company?'

Henrietta replied, unperturbed, 'Mama will be so pleased. We are all invited to dine on board *L'Ésperance*. Just think, Rose.' She waited until Rose's head moved a fraction back towards her. 'What an opportunity. I told him that you are considered to be the most accomplished young lady in the colony. We had such a long conversation about it. I am sure the baron means his invitation as a way to be able to spend more time with you.'

Chapter 5

Always welcome at the Palace

The prospect of dining on board the French ship, *L'Ésperance,* had put them all in fine humour. De Bougainville ushered them about the vessel, and Beth was captivated by everything she saw. *Perhaps it's the sight of so many uniforms, or perhaps it's the presence of the baron himself,* she pondered. He was taller than any other man on board, and his broad shoulders were accentuated by the large epaulettes on his coat.

Mr Burbridge delighted in the tour about the ship, admiring the fit-out. The Burbridges were part-owners of one ship, *The Kinsmen,* and this ownership status rendered Mr Burbridge as a self-acclaimed expert in matters of shipping. Baron de Bougainville was too well bred to call him out.

Griffith, who was indeed a highly experienced seaman, had been unable to join them. In his place, Bill had come along after some persuasion—he had little tolerance for 'froggies', as he called them; in fact, he had little tolerance for anyone not of British origin. He was also the least ocean-going of all the Burbridges, preferring the solid ground and to have the bush about him. Mr Burbridge, therefore, was able to hold the floor so that even the commodore barely had the opportunity to speak.

It was then only to be expected that de Bougainville paid particular attention to the ladies of the party as soon as they were seated to dine.

'Your French is excellent, madame,' he commented to Mrs Burbridge.

'My dear father was French. He was of the de Perroquets of Dauphiné.'

'So how does the daughter of a distinguished Frenchman come to find herself in this remote part of the world?'

Mrs Burbridge continued, 'My father left France and successfully established himself as a merchant in Calcutta. My mother was introduced to him by Baroness von Imhoff, who was by then the wife of Governor Hastings. My mother was a great favourite of the Hastings, you know,' Mrs Burbridge preened. 'Always welcome at the Palace.'

Beth could see that de Bougainville's eyes were glazing over as her mother talked on, but he maintained his polite expression of attention through the *Potage Tortue*.

'My mother had lived in India since she was a young child of five, having been adopted by Hasting's aide-de camp Colonel White and his wife. Her own family—'

With the serving of the *Saumon a` la Royale*, Mrs Burbridge's account of her family history was interrupted by Henrietta. 'You would have visited Chandanagore, perhaps, in one of your many voyages?' she asked de Bougainville in French.

De Bougainville followed the change in topic with alacrity, and soon he and his officers were regaling their guests with tall tales from their voyages, while Henrietta deftly challenged and teased them all. Richeley's face was flushed. It might have been the wine—so far, they'd been offered sherry with their soup, and hock with the fish, and Richeley had not been content with only one glass per course. Henrietta's enjoyment of the conversation was obviously adding to his consumption.

'But you have had many adventures yourself?' de Bougainville asked. 'Mr Richeley and yourself have travelled widely in India, as I understand it.'

Richeley took a generous sip of wine in preparation for making a contribution, but Henrietta was there before him.

'Well, bandits did add a certain frisson to journeying through West Bengal by boat,' she said.

She had the attention of all the officers.

'It was baking hot, with a fiery wind rattling at the flimsy blinds as if to mock our meagre efforts to withstand heat of the coming monsoon.' Her voice became serious. 'We had sepoys on board throughout the trip from Calcutta to Agra, with replacement shifts coming on and off at every military station we passed. Early in the journey, we'd hear them on deck playing cards, but as we moved northward they stayed grim and alert. One night, there came a great splashing and shouting. I peered out the window. From the deck, shots burst into the inky blackness. Then I saw them. Dacoits, the glint of their knives held in their teeth, their dark naked bodies, oiled to slip from the soldiers' grips, sliding up out of the water to gain purchase on the deck.'

There was an audible gasp from Ducampier, which made his fellow officers laugh, though they too had stayed the movement of their forks to their mouths, caught in Henrietta's tale.

'And so we scared the cheeky blighters off,' Richeley broke in.

The serving of champagne signalled the arrival of the *Chaud Froid de Volaille*. Conversations among the diners fell to general topics such as the food, the state of the colony, and the officers' views on everything they'd seen. Ducampier was paying particular attention to Rose, who looked none too pleased about it. Rose, who had fended off unwanted suitors since she was barely fifteen, nodded at the officer's comments and maintained a stony face unless de Bougainville spoke, whereupon her eyes lit up.

When they had first arrived, Beth had thought that the baron's eye had dwelt on Rose with pleasure, though once Henrietta had come aboard, he had looked at little else. His gaze was intense as he listened to her.

'The tiger cubs were no bigger than my hand, as I reached in to pet them,' Henrietta was saying.

'And did you not have fears for your life, Madame Richeley,' de Bougainville asked. 'Where was the mother of these charming cubs?'

'Oh, she was away hunting,' Henrietta said airily. Then she added, her voice lowered for effect, 'My guide was a little worried that I tarried so long, but really how could anyone tear themselves away from such a sight?'

By the arrival of the *Pouding aux Amandes, à l'eau à l'orange*, Mrs Burbridge was darting outraged looks between de Bougainville and Henrietta. As Richeley's face purpled, even the other officers showed signs of being disconcerted. Ducampier, as Master of *L'Ésperance*, suggested abruptly that the men take their brandy and cigars out on deck.

As soon as they'd left, Mrs Burbridge rounded upon Henrietta.

'Lively conversation is one thing, Henrietta, but frank flirtation is highly inappropriate—particularly for a married woman.'

'On the contrary, Mama,' said Henrietta, 'flirtation in an unmarried lady might be open to misconstruction, and therefore attract social opprobrium, but the same behaviour can be recognised as entirely innocent for a married one.'

'But what might the commodore be thinking of you?'

'A lot, I hope,' Henrietta's lips twitched.

Chapter 6

Time is all, my friend

Beth had thought that they would see the baron soon after dining on *L'Ésperance*—it was spring after all, and the roads were passable, and the first parties and soirées of the season had begun. They responded to so many invitations that Richeley began to complain that he would never conclude his business so he and Henrietta could depart.

And the way Rose did nothing but sigh whenever de Bougainville's name was mentioned didn't help her relationship with Henrietta. After one week, Henrietta began to tease Rose mercilessly. However, after two weeks, Henrietta ignored Rose and instead developed an interest in the building of the Burbridge's new villa.

As the days passed, Henrietta seemed to be trying hard to be nicer to her husband. She even smiled benignly when he disappeared with the gentlemen for more port, leaving her to chat with the ladies.

At Henrietta's suggestion, Beth joined her for a walk down towards the river in the spring sunshine. Henrietta paused to pick one of the first blooms from the rhododendron she'd planted four years before. She plucked at the petals, pollen scattering over her palms. She tried to brush off the yellow grains, but they were sticky and clung in little specks to her skin. The lush red of the flower shone in the morning sun.

Henrietta gave a start, catching sight of a yawl as it tacked its way along the river. It made good headway, even though the breeze was light. It was headed to their jetty, and Henrietta walked down towards it, her step quickening and outpacing Beth. The yawl was close, but they couldn't see who was sailing it—his face hidden by the dipping sails. With a sharp flap of canvas, the boat came about, and they could finally see him.

The baron leapt effortlessly from the boat. 'Madame Richeley,' he said with a deep bow. 'Forgive me for arriving unannounced. I was on my way back to Sydney from the governor's residence at Parramatta and thought to stop and pay my respects. I did not think to have a welcome party.'

'It is not so special as all that,' replied Henrietta. 'You know that I wait here at this very spot all day, every day, just to be welcoming. It is my vocation.'

Beth could see the translation in his eyes—then he laughed. 'In that case, I am indeed the most fortunate of men to have been the first to be welcomed today.' He barely glanced at Beth as they slowly walked up to the house.

At Mrs Burbridge's insistence, the baron was prevailed upon to be shown about the estate and then to dine with the family. He showed little resistance, charming Mr Burbridge with his interest in every

aspect of the property and delighting Mrs Burbridge
with his attentions to her daughters. The only person
proof against his charms was Richeley, who found his
way to the claret with alarming frequency.

'Captain Rossi tells me that you'll be setting out on
the next leg of your journey very soon,' said Richeley.

'We were to leave next week, but I have decided
that we should remain a while longer. There is much of
interest here.' De Bougainville was looking at Henrietta
as he spoke. He added, 'And you and Mrs Richeley will
be also leaving soon, I hear?'

'Yes, very soon,' Richeley answered, gesturing to
Susan to refill his glass. 'There are a few loose ends to
tie off. I've got a hundred head of cattle sitting up
Paterson way that are to be moved by Bill to market,
and well, then we'll be set.'

'I told you, it can't be for at least another month,'
said Bill.

'Time is all, my friend,' said Richeley, tapping the
side of his nose with his finger.

'You will enjoy the journey back to Calcutta, Mrs
Richeley?' the baron asked.

The fact that the baron had directed his attention to
Henrietta for a second time drew frowns from Rose.
'Oh, my sister adores sea voyages—as do I,' Rose said.

'Weren't you seasick the whole way from England,
little sister?' teased Bill. 'I'm sure we didn't see your

tiny head emerge on deck unless we were stopped at port.'

'Travelling by sea is a fine thing,' said Henrietta. 'But first class, of course, and preferably with one's own servant.' She looked pointedly at her husband.

Richeley shook his head. 'Quite what the fairer members of our species need that cannot be satisfied with the attentions of the cabin stewards, is beyond me.'

'When I returned four years ago, I should have thought to bring my ayah with me, then I'd have her for the return trip.'

Mrs Burbridge muttered, 'You have made good use of Tyler to remedy that gap while you've been here.'

'Perhaps Tyler might—' Henrietta broke off at the expression on Mrs Burbridge's face.

'That young maid I had sent up to me, what's her name?' said Bill. 'Sarah something? She's not settling in at all well. I'll let you have her.'

Henrietta's eyes narrowed. 'What exactly do you mean by "not settling in"?'

Mrs Burbridge, who had been trying to head off this domestic conversation for some time, finally succeeded. 'If we're all finished, I wonder if I might suggest a game of cards? Loo, perhaps?'

There was a noisy scraping of furniture as people rose from dinner. Mr Burbridge, who had barely said a word through the meal, disappeared into the study with Bill.

'Baron de Bougainville?' Mrs Burbridge asked. 'Do you play?'

Rose interrupted, asking, 'I wonder if now would be a good time for me to show you those drawings of the grevillea family I was telling you about?'

The baron looked distracted. 'Yes, yes, of course, for my report.' He followed her over to the far table near the window where the light was best.

Beth agreed to cards without much enthusiasm. Henrietta was a shrewd player and regularly took the pot, while Richeley's playing was impetuous and unsuccessful. The game proceeded quietly for a while, but then on his third chance to win the trick, Richeley turned over his card but it failed to trump Beth's card.

'Never mind, Mr Richeley,' said Mrs Burbridge. 'Time to put in your loo.'

'I hadn't moved yet. Pass,' replied Richeley.

Henrietta, who was ahead in the game, demanded, 'Come on, pay up.'

Beth, embarrassed, drew a piece of paper towards her. 'Perhaps I could make a note, if you'd prefer?'

Richeley threw his cards on the table. 'I said, pass. If you're going to accuse me of cheating, then I'm out of the game.' He looked over at Rose and the baron. 'Aren't you two lovebirds finished yet?' he said, his speech slurred. He helped himself again from the decanter.

'Another game of loo, Mr Richeley?' Beth asked uncertainly.

Henrietta shuffled the cards with a sharp snap.

Richeley rubbed his forehead. 'Forgive me,' he said, rising to his feet. 'A slight headache. I might take the air on the verandah for a short while, if you'll excuse me.'

Rose's cheeks still flushed in reaction to Richeley's comment about herself and de Bougainville, and she had ceased her explanation of her catalogue of drawings. 'Captain Piper says he wants to hold a ball in your honour,' she said. 'I do hope you won't be leaving before then?'

The baron looked over to Henrietta. Perhaps he saw the answer in her eyes, since he answered, 'A ball, in my honour, how could I not attend?'

Chapter 7

So many opportunities for scandal

The laughter of the guests was high and bright in anticipation of the evening.

'How did you come?'

'Oh, by the sloop, of course. The harbour provides such a pretty way to approach the Point.'

'The best view of the villa and all the lights, I agree.'

With the arrival of guests from each successive carriage, barge and sloop, the large rooms and manicured gardens of the Vaucluse House were filling with every citizen of any consequence in the colony.

'No, no,' Mrs Burbridge answered someone's enquiry. 'We're staying in town tonight.'

As usual, she had quickly been surrounded by a cluster of the leading matrons of the town.

'By far the best solution, really.' She then went on. 'Mr Burbridge is most keen to attend the race days.'

'I couldn't agree more. Why, the last time we attended one of Captain Piper's entertainments we didn't get home until ...'

Ahead, Governor Brisbane stood in the reception line with Captain Piper to greet the guests as they arrived. Captain Piper's wife, being the daughter of a convict, was not present, but Mrs Brisbane did the honours of hostess for the evening. Beth caught snatches of gossip as friends caught up.

'She could have made a far more respectable match.'

'I really don't see why he had to actually marry her … he wouldn't have been the first to …'

'Did you see, Mr Justice Wood's here … up ahead with young Mary. I can't see Mrs Wood.'

'It's not like Mrs Wood to miss an occasion like this.'

'Well, nothing would keep Mr Giles Wood away. He needs to be seen in society if he's to have a chance at replacing Chief Justice Ferris when he retires.'

Beth tugged at her gloves, her fingers worrying the button at her wrist. She should have worn her white ones, she realised, looking around at the other ladies. She was conscious too of the cool evening air across her skin that was exposed by the square-cut neckline of her dress. She wished she were older and could wear a lace bertha like her mother.

'Burbridge, old man, delighted to see you,' Mr Campbell said. 'And I haven't had a chance to congratulate your son, here.' He clapped Bill on the back. 'That route you found through to Wollombi is going to save us all a lot of time and money.'

Bill nodded in acknowledgement, tugging at his collar as if it had suddenly become too tight.

Mr Campbell continued, 'Another explorer in the Burbridge family—taking after your Uncle Herbert—well done, well done.'

Mr Burbridge interrupted his effusions. 'Interested in the race, Campbell? I'm getting up a party. Bill here will be coming along, of course.'

'And Griffith,' Bill added.

Griffith turned at his name, pausing in his conversation with Mr Justice Wood.

Mr Burbridge awkwardly waved an arm as if to include them both in his invitation.

As much as her father disliked Mr Justice Wood's politics, Beth saw he couldn't resist the opportunity to emphasise a connection with the judiciary, even if their association was through their wives' friendship.

'I'm afraid it will depend on how the case before me tomorrow unfolds but, of course, my thanks for your invitation,' Mr Justice Wood replied courteously.

Mr Burbridge continued without acknowledging the interruption, 'And of course, Baron de Bougainville is keen to see how our equine events compare.'

Mr Campbell hesitated.

Mr McPhail smiled nervously. 'I'll be there, of course. Sir John has insisted I see that new filly of his get put through her paces.'

Mr Campbell still hadn't answered.

There was an uncomfortable pause, broken only by the bustle when the line began to move up the stairs and Mr Burbridge was forced back a step lower.

The line continued to edge them closer to the governor.

Beth watched her father nervously. He had spent most of their journey here ranting about yet another thing the governor had done to stymie progress in the colony. As this was the usual state of affairs between her father and successive governors, Beth had paid little heed. But what if he vented his spleen here, with everyone around? All she wanted was a quiet evening where she could talk with as few people as possible. Her shoulders hunched to shrink her to invisibility.

Two steps more and her father was before Governor Brisbane. Beth caught the governor's swift change of expression to one of resignation. She felt a stab of shame that her father should feel so much and yet elicit mere dismissal.

Reaching Mrs Brisbane was like finding an oasis of calm. She always had a smile and a kind word despite the vexations of her public role.

She greeted Mrs Burbridge with enthusiasm. 'Ladies Committee meeting next week,' she said. 'Not that I need to remind you,' she said as if the two were conspirators.

From beside her, Captain Piper said jocularly, 'There won't be a dissolute female convict left in the colony after all of your ladies have done with them.' His broad smile stretched to his ears as he greeted Henrietta. 'Mrs Richeley. And, don't tell me, Mr Richeley too,' he added. His feigned surprise was obviously entirely for show, since he had explicitly invited them both. 'How is your little Eliza? Have you brought her along?'

'She's still a little young, Captain Piper,' said Henrietta. 'But I am under strict instructions to send you her love.'

'Pity, pity. She is a delightful child.' He turned to Mrs Brisbane. 'Have I ever told you the story of little Eliza's adventures?'

Mrs Burbridge smiled. 'You were quite the hero, Captain Piper.'

Henrietta's smile became fixed. Richeley looked blankly from one to the other.

'Imagine, Mrs Brisbane. A wee mite, barely two years old—'

'Three,' Henrietta said under her breath.

'And struck low with dysentery, journeying all the way from Calcutta to Sydney in a servant's care.' Henrietta's mouth was open as if to explain, but Captain Piper continued without pause. 'As soon as her ship entered the harbour, I took her on to my own boat and—'

'And the first we knew about it,' said Mrs Burbridge, 'was when we heard the music coming up the river—'

'My band, you know.'

'And there came Captain Piper walking up our lawn, bearing little Eliza in his arms to give her to me.'

Captain Piper was still chuckling at the memory when the press of the line meant that the Burbridges had to move along and out into the ballroom.

The room was so large that even though there might have been more than fifty people there already, they clustered about the sides as if afraid to take the centre of the dance floor too early. The high domed cupola at the end of the room made the space even more cavernous, and its arches were echoed in the curved niches with statuary along the sides. More arches opened into wide halls and rooms branching out to other parts of the villa. The tall French windows at the far end looked out to the sloping gardens and the harbour beyond.

Beth felt the plainness of her gown all the more in this setting of grandeur. One of the archways framed the musicians from the Band of the Buffs, whose brass buttons on their regimental uniforms shone as brightly as their polished instruments. She stood in the far corner of the room as she waited for her mother to stop mingling and settle in a chair with the other matrons so that she too could retire to a seat nearby.

'Come on, Beth,' begged Rose, linking her arm through hers. 'Baron de Bougainville has arrived and I can't be seen to greet him alone.'

At the sound of the baron's name, Henrietta had turned, but Richeley took her elbow and steered her in the direction of his friend Captain Rossi, the superintendent of the police.

Beth couldn't get out of her mind the look on the governor's face when greeting her father. Mr Burbridge was still by the entrance to the room as she let Rose steer her through the groups of chatting guests. He was talking earnestly to Baron de Bougainville and Captain Ducamper.

'And Sir John has a fine filly that'll be racing, I hear,' Mr Burbridge was saying.

At the sisters' approach, the baron looked relieved.

When the band started up, Baron de Bougainville asked Rose to dance. Beth wondered if this reaction might be less to do with any fascination that Rose might be eliciting, and more to do with the possibility of escaping the tedium of conversation with her father.

She stayed beside her father as he continued to talk with Captain Ducamper, who showed no inclination to join the dancing. She watched de Bougainville lead Rose onto the floor to take their places for the minuet. Rose was looking at her best—the green silk of her dress glistened in the light from the chandelier above. Her complexion glowed against the deep brown of her hair, which was arranged in clustered ringlets about her cheeks. *They make an arresting couple.* The baron's handsome face bowed with interest at something Rose had said. Beth wasn't the only one in the room to watch them. Every spinster in the room followed their movements, and maternal eyes narrowed shrewdly. Rose would have to work hard to have another opportunity to dance with the baron.

When the set ended, the baron was whisked away by Mrs Hawkins and steered in the direction of her daughter. However, Rose's eyes were bright with happiness when she returned to Beth's side.

'If I had to leave the ball now, I would leave happy,' she said.

Baron de Bougainville was over the other side of the room, dancing with Miss Hawkins, but as Rose caught his eye he smiled, bowing his head a fraction in acknowledgement.

'Oh, Beth.' Rose was clearly too excited to speak.

Mrs Burbridge had finally settled with her coterie of friends on seats far away from the orchestra so as to hear themselves gossip. Henrietta and Griffith were chatting with Miss Mary Wood and her father. Bill stood slightly off to one side. He stretched his shoulders every so often, his heavy shoulders straining at the fabric of his suit.

'Miss Burbridge and Miss Beth,' said Mr Justice Wood, his smile genuinely warm as they joined them. 'You are both looking in fine health. I'm afraid we won't be staying long. Mrs Wood is poorly and frets if I am away too long.'

At Mary's look of disappointment, and with the encouragement of Griffith's elbow, Henrietta spoke. 'Perhaps we could keep an eye on Miss Wood if she would like to stay a little longer. I'm sure Father would have no objection to us returning her home.'

When Mr Justice Wood took his leave, Griffith and Mary exchanged delighted glances. The three sisters turned to make their way to where their mother sat. However, they hadn't gone more than a couple of steps before Baron de Bougainville was before them. He bowed deeply, kissing Henrietta's hand.

'Mrs Richeley, a delight to see you once more. How is it that your husband has let you out of his sight? Surely, as interesting as Captain Rossi is, he cannot compete with your attractions?'

Rose was barely hiding the venom as she stared at Henrietta.

'And we will not have you with us for very much longer, I gather?' Griffith asked de Bougainville.

'No, sadly, *c'est vrai*. But even a few days are something to remember, *n'est-ce pas*? But, we cannot tarry much longer.'

'Unlike our intrepid commander's last sojourn in the wilds of Botany Bay so many years ago,' said Captain Ducamper, who had joined them.

'My second-in-command is determined to embarrass me with the imputation of my having a disreputable past.' De Bougainville smiled at Mary, who was looking to Griffith as if seeking a translation.

'I do not think that scandal is unfamiliar to the denizens of Sydney,' Captain Ducamper returned the sally. 'Look about us.' He gestured to the ballroom at large. 'Such closeness between the dancing couples. So many opportunities for scandal.' He looked as if he relished the idea.

Griffith laughed. 'Just wait—the waltzes will be next.'

'No, no,' cried Captain Ducamper, rolling his eyes. 'If a quadrille is so inspiring, imagine what the novelty of the waltz may do.'

They had all been so absorbed in their conversation that they had forgotten the presence of the other people nearby.

Mrs McPhail leaned in. 'Oh, we're perfectly modern, I assure you. Waltzing is not at all uncommon these days. You can back me up, can't you, Mrs Richeley?'

'Did I hear you mention the waltz?' asked Mr McPhail. 'A most unsociable sort of dance.'

Captain Ducamper shook his head. 'How can you say that?'

Mr McPhail pronounced sternly, 'With a quadrille, you are being sociable with many people, whereas with a waltz, you are being exclusive.'

'And perhaps rather too sociable in that way,' contributed Mrs Hawkins, glaring at her daughter as if she had committed the sin of waltzing.

Mr McPhail harrumphed his agreement.

Mrs McPhail went on bravely. 'But the papers report the waltz is danced at royal balls, at St James' Palace, no less. Surely, that means we may do so.' She looked to Henrietta in appeal.

'Perhaps, like all dances, any offence might lie in how it is danced,' Henrietta said, clearly with care. 'After all, a mazurka can be rough and alarming if the gentleman is insufficiently sensitive to his partner.'

Mr McPhail and Mrs Hawkins began speaking at once, arguing about the dangers of various forms of dancing.

'So, Captain Ducamper, you were right to say that dancing leads to scandal,' said Griffith. 'Why, even the mention of the word waltz is enough to fire up a debate.'

'Well, it's Captain Ducamper's fault for bringing up the topic of waltzing,' said Mrs McPhail.

'That's because of the way the officers dance,' blurted Miss Wood, who then looked swiftly to her feet, obviously overcome with having spoken.

'Not all officers, I hope, and never with a young lady such as yourself,' said Griffith gallantly.

Bill, who had barely spoken all night, whispered loudly to Captain Ducamper, 'I hear that in the mess, they call the waltz, "verandah screening".' He smiled broadly as though pleased at being able to contribute a *bon mot*.

Thankfully, de Bougainville made the effort to steer the topic into safer waters. 'Well, we can't blame dancing, with all its perils, for every scandal in the world. Scandals happen all the time, even when the dancing is over,' he said.

For all his effort, Beth was relieved when the serving of supper was announced. It was well past midnight and the lateness of the hour meant that there was a crush towards the food.

In the melée, Baron de Bougainville ended up escorting Miss Hawkins into supper, followed by Captain Ducamper with a disgruntled Rose.

Mrs Burbridge took Mr Burbridge's arm. 'I'm sure Mr Richeley will want to accompany you, if you wait,' she said pointedly to Henrietta.

Beth stood by the archway with Henrietta. They could catch glimpses of the table close to collapse under the weight of the fare put before the guests. As well as the usual cold ham, turkey and sandwiches, there was poached salmon, mounds of beans, carrots, mushrooms and potatoes. If guests still had sufficient room, they could indulge in the garishly decorated cakes, biscuits, pastries and jellies. Beth was faintly queasy. Perhaps, if she ever made it as far as the table, she'd opt for a small selection of fruits and cheeses.

'Supper is the last thing on Richeley's mind,' Henrietta muttered, linking her arm through Beth's and steering them towards the supper. 'Captain Rossi and his cronies will have him at cards. Or at least, I hope it's cards.'

'Cards did you say?' Bill headed away towards the far hall, still bearing a full plate of food.

Mrs Burbridge emerged from the throng about the table, her plate sparsely filled. 'Captain Piper's suppers are so very fine,' she commented to Mrs McPhail, eyeing her loaded plate.

'Do you have sufficient, Mama?' Rose had detached herself from Captain Ducamper but, if she had hoped this might leave her arm free for de Bougainville, she was unsuccessful. He was surrounded by admirers.

'Dearest Rose, you are so very good to me. I can't think what I will do without you,' Mrs Burbridge said.

Mrs McPhail looked at her with a gleam of interest. 'So then, you think there might be a prospect of …?' She let her voice trail off significantly.

'No, no, pay me no mind,' said Mrs Burbridge. 'Marriage is such a complex decision, isn't it?' Her gaze flicked sharply from Rose to where Griffith was assisting Mary Wood to fill her plate, despite her protestations. 'Did I tell you that Mr Burbridge's niece back in Kent has announced her engagement? To a fine handsome man, about Griffith's age, I gather. His friends call him "The Lady Killer".'

'No,' exclaimed Mrs McPhail.

'This will be his third marriage,' Mrs Burbridge said in a low voice.

'Really?' Mrs McPhail leaned forward to hear more.

The two women were quickly engrossed.

Baron de Bougainville appeared in front of Henrietta and Beth. 'Mrs Richeley?' he asked.

Without another word, Henrietta took his outstretched hand and they vanished out to the main ballroom where the sounds of the waltz had begun.

Beth had thought that de Bougainville and Rose attracted many an admiring glance, but as she moved to the archway from where she could see the dancing, that was nothing to the sight of de Bougainville and Henrietta. He held her close to his body, their postures aligned, their movements in complete synchrony. Henrietta's height allowed their eyes to lock as they danced. Her dress was a deep gold silk, her bodice cut low and off the shoulders. Her garnets flashed about her neck, the gold chain catching and re-catching the light as her bosom rose and fell with the exertion of the dance. Her arms appeared almost bare, as her short, puffed sleeves served merely to attach the sheer skin-tight oversleeves that stretched to her delicate lace gloves.

It was hard to look away. Many a conversation in the onlookers lapsed until the set was over. After a momentary hush, the buzz resumed. Beth lost sight of them as the other couples on the dance floor moved apart and returned to their friends. She then finally saw them standing by the long windows that led out to the gardens, staring into each other's eyes. In unison, they turned and went out into the night.

'Have you eaten, Beth?' Mrs Burbridge rose to her feet. 'Well, as I'm always telling you ...'

But Beth wasn't listening. In fact, she had barely eaten at all. She had eaten so little in the past weeks—months really—that her ball gown gaped under the arms and across the décolletage. It had taken all Susan's ingenuity to disguise the poor fit. But the cramping in her stomach wasn't hunger. Her thoughts spun from Rose's efforts through the evening to garner de Bougainville's attention, to Henrietta, loitering in the balmy night air, the lights in the garden sparkling across the water, and de Bougainville ...

Confused, she followed Mrs McPhail and her mother as they began to walk around the room. Her mother was waylaid by Mrs Brisbane, and Mrs McPhail paused to talk with others of her acquaintance. Beth scanned the room for any sight of Rose.

'Well, you know what the governor said when Mr Burbridge's name got put forward, don't you?' Mrs McPhail was talking with the woman on her right, clearly unaware that Beth was still in earshot.

She didn't want to hear what Mrs McPhail was about to say. She wanted to flee but she couldn't face the supper room—it was only a matter of time before her mother asked her where Henrietta was. And she couldn't go out into the garden where Henrietta and de Bougainville …

'Mr McPhail has it from Mr Campbell.' Mrs McPhail dropped her voice into a whisper. 'Apparently,' she continued, 'the governor said …' Mrs McPhail glanced over her shoulder and, seeing Beth, her colour heightened—but the way her mouth pursed suggested that Beth was somehow at fault for eavesdropping.

All Beth knew was that she had to leave. Her father—she should find him and say she was ill, and he'd organise for a carriage. She strode through the crowded room, the intensity of her expression parting the way for her.

She found him standing on the edge of a crowd of gentlemen smoking cigars. He wasn't talking—his conversational style was so slow and ponderous that others with faster tongues would always manage to speak first. She tried to catch his eye. His face was ruddy and his hair looked like he'd run his hand through it in exasperation. Standing as he was at the periphery, he looked like the man he really was—a short, stout farmer from Kent.

Chapter 8

Never was a boat named more aptly

Beth couldn't sleep. When she heard Rose enter the room, she closed her eyes. Rose's movements about the room were quick and agitated. She brushed her hair so fast and for so long that the strands crackled. Finally, she lay down, the hotel bed creaking with each toss and turn until finally she lay still. Careful not to disturb her, Beth wrapped her shawl about her shoulders and crept out onto the hotel landing and over to the far window. The innkeeper had left it wide open to welcome the slightest breeze.

The street below was almost empty. The full moon cast a ghostly glow across the boards traversing the worst of the potholes in the dirt roadway. At the corner, two bare feet stuck out from under a loaded barrow amid a pile of old blankets, the sleeper guarding his wares. Three mangy dogs, their skin taut across their ribs, slunk the length of the street on a mission to hunt.

Then from the other corner, two figures sauntered—a man and a woman, leaning into each other as they walked, neither entirely steady. They stopped and the man drew the woman's face close, his palm cradling her cheek, his fingers reaching into her hair, and he kissed her. Finally, the woman broke the embrace. Her throaty laugh sounded softly in the stillness.

Henrietta.

Beth had thought Henrietta would have come back with Rose and her parents. But she was with de Bougainville—for Beth recognised him now, the wide shoulders of his uniform were enough to identify him as they came closer.

The couple, entwined again, had reached the hotel. But the doors were all locked, Beth realised. She drew back in the darkness. But something must have alerted Henrietta, since she looked up at Beth. Henrietta mimed going around to the side door and took a couple of steps in that direction, only for de Bougainville to draw her back into him, hunching over her, his face crushed to her neck.

Beth felt the heat rise through her, as if the window was the open brazier of the blacksmith's forge. She leapt back, scalded. She ran down the stairs and through the dark service corridor. There was a red glow at the end from the last embers of the kitchen fire and she went towards it to find her way into the kitchen. Under her bare feet, the flagstones were cold. There was a gentle tap at the door, and Beth eased the bolts back.

De Bougainville had gone and Henrietta stood alone swaying slightly. She stepped in, grasping the sides of the door for balance. Beth slid the bolts back into position.

Henrietta grasped Beth's hands. 'Midnight tomorrow,' she whispered. 'Just think.' Her eyes glowed with the red of the coals.

'What?' Beth couldn't collect her thoughts. She had seen her sister … she'd seen her … it was an act too intimate to witness. It was inconceivable that Henrietta could … 'What?' she repeated stupidly.

'On *L'Ésperance*,' Henrietta said, far too loudly. 'Never was a boat named more aptly.'

Chapter 9

May I have a moment, Mama

Breakfast had been set up for the family in a small private parlour of the hotel. The sideboard was laden with mutton chops, blood sausage, boiled eggs, fried potatoes, tomatoes and fruit. The day was warming up too quickly for the fish to be kept out of the kitchen's cellar for long. As each member of the family entered, Susan set about liaising with the hotel kitchen for their order.

The blinds had been drawn against the sun since early morning, but by the time Beth entered the room, it was stifling. By the look of him, Mr Burbridge had slept ill—his eyes were bloodshot and pouchy. He glared at her but didn't speak. Beth knew that her leaving early was one among the many things that had displeased him from the previous evening. She placed a small nectarine on a plate and sat to eat it.

'And that's all you're going to have?' Mrs Burbridge asked Beth. 'The number of times I was asked if you were unwell last night ...'

'Can't a man have a little peace and quiet while he eats?' Mr Burbridge grumbled.

Mrs Burbridge continued her breakfast calmly as if she hadn't heard.

When Rose joined them, their father's temper was still brewing.

'Shall I order more tea, Mama?' Rose offered, feeling the side of the silver teapot.

'Yes, you are such a dear.'

When Susan had disappeared to carry out the implied order, Mrs Burbridge continued, 'You looked lovely last night, Rose. So many gentlemen looking in your direction. You and the baron made such a handsome couple in the minuet.'

Mr Burbridge grunted derisively.

'What ever do you mean by that, Mr Burbridge? I thought you approved of the baron?' Mrs Burbridge asked.

'The chap had the hide to renege on the races. At the last minute too, as he was leaving Piper's last night. Other plans, he said.'

Rose looked thoughtful. 'Well, he doesn't have much longer here.' She sounded as if she was trying to convince herself of something. 'He needs to make the most of every opportunity ...'

'Happy to waste his time flirting with everything in a skirt, though,' Mr Burbridge mumbled.

Mrs Burbridge, clearly seeing Rose's look of alarm, tried to return to her theme. 'Well, you drew every eye,

Rose. Why, even though Mr Justice Wood could stay only a short time, he clearly made a special effort to talk with you.'

'Wood. Don't tell me your schemes have stooped so low.' The cutlery jumped as Mr Burbridge pounded his fist on the table. 'His wife's still alive, isn't she? And, even if she weren't, why, the man's a complete Whig.'

'But I thought you'd asked him to come along with you and the boys to the races?' Mrs Burbridge looked bewildered.

Beth, by dint of slowly peeling the delicate skin of the nectarine and eating it in thin slivers, attempted to appear to be eating a breakfast.

She'd spent the rest of the night, lying prone on the bed, the sheets damp with sweat beneath her. Rose had done her best to attract de Bougainville. But Mama had charged her with keeping Henrietta from flirting with de Bougainville.

It's all my fault.

Beth went to the sideboard and poured herself a cup of lukewarm tea. She proceeded to take tiny sips to make it last. She had to decide what to do.

She didn't want to interfere. She had never in her life interfered—not with Papa's plans, not with Mama's schemes. But then, if Rose had accepted one of her many other previous suitors, there would never have been any need to attract him in the first place. It didn't seem to matter to Mama or Papa when Rose turned down yet another suitor for this or that reason, which was of no account. Mama still gushed over her and called her 'dearest Rose'. Beth had held her tongue—she'd tried to keep their home orderly and quiet and harmonious. She had done her best. But now, everything had changed.

Rose might have thought that de Bougainville would fall for her charms as so many others had, but Beth doubted it. To be sure, his eyes shone with appreciation of Rose's beauty, but Beth couldn't see anything beyond that. She could barely express what it was that was missing, even to herself.

And that brought her back to Henrietta.

She tried not to think about what she'd witnessed last night. But it all came back to Henrietta—all the discord and upset. *How can Henrietta possibly think she can fulfil a promise for a midnight assignation on a boat in the harbour?* Not much happened in the colony that others didn't find out about, and there was nothing the little society liked better than a scandal.

And Papa's efforts to receive the respect he deserved were thwarted again and again. Beth pushed back the memory of the slights she'd overheard last night. He was the sort of gentleman this colony needed. Last night, she'd considered going straight to her father, but it only took a moment's reflection for her to know she didn't have the courage.

There was a quiet tap at the door and Susan ushered in one of the hotel staff with freshly made tea.

Susan cleared her throat nervously and held out a note. 'Delivered from Carter Lodge, Mr Burbridge.'

He read it through hurriedly and screwed the paper into a ball.

'What is it?' asked Mrs Burbridge.

'Wood—pleading the pressures of office and giving his apologies for the races. Ridiculous.' He stood and tossed his napkin aside. He grunted at Henrietta by way of greeting her arrival on his way out.

'Henrietta,' said Mrs Burbridge, raising her eyebrows reprovingly. 'Good afternoon.'

'It's not quite that late, Mama,' said Henrietta. 'Can you get me a glass of warm milk, Susan?' She examined the sideboard briefly and then took a seat without filling a plate. Henrietta looked paler than usual, but it gave her an ethereal air, emphasising the translucency of her complexion rather than detracting from it.

Rose looked at Henrietta coldly; however, her expression shifted to one of sweetness when she said, 'Mama, do you think we should visit poor Mrs Wood later today?'

'That's very thoughtful of you, dearest. Yes, indeed, I think we should.'

'So kind of you, Rose,' said Henrietta. 'But I don't think Mr Justice Wood will be there. The court is in session, isn't it?'

Rose flushed with anger.

'Well, I must say, Henrietta has found you out, Rose,' said Mrs Burbridge.

The chat and teasing went on until Beth thought she'd never get a chance to speak with her mother alone. It was the only way. At worst, she might at least be able to raise some questions in her mother's mind. And at best, her mother would find a way to manage to prevent the assignation discretely.

Eventually, Henrietta and Rose left, neither making eye contact with the other.

'May I speak with you, Mama?' Beth asked.

Her mother looked querulous. 'Will it take long? I do have rather a lot to be going on with.'

'I think it may be important.'

Mrs Burbridge sat down again and waited.

'There's, well, I think there's to be an assignation ...' Beth couldn't organise her thoughts. It was all coming out in a jumble. She tried again. 'With de Bougainville.'

Mrs Burbridge looked delighted. 'Well, that's good news. Will he be at the Wood's too?'

'No, that's the thing. I think they may be meeting, alone.'

Mrs Burbridge frowned. 'Are you sure?'

Now that it had come to it, Beth found herself unable to go on.

Mrs Burbridge patted her hand. 'There, there. I think you may have mistaken matters.' Her tone was that to a child. 'Dearest Rose wouldn't think of such a thing.' Mrs Burbridge shifted her chair as though to rise.

'But it's Henrietta,' said Beth. She quailed before the look her mother gave her. She took a deep breath and blurted, 'Midnight. Henrietta has an assignation with Baron de Bougainville on board *L'Ésperance.*'

'Tonight?' Finally, Mrs Burbridge grasped the totality of Beth's news.

Beth nodded her head mutely.

Chapter 10

She's gone, Miss Beth

Her mother came in without knocking.

Beth couldn't remember the last time her mother had come into her room when she was the sole occupant. If Rose were with her, then Mama would often come in to find out what they were talking about or to join in the gossip. But, as soon as Rose left, so did Mama.

'I little thought when I suggested that you stay close by Henrietta, that you would uncover such a situation,' Mrs Burbridge said. 'I wanted to say that your father and I are most grateful.' She swallowed, as if the words of thanks were sticking in her gullet.

Beth hung onto the words of gratitude, though they were few enough. A day before, such words would have brought her joy but, now that they had come, they were like a shell left behind when abandoned—just an empty relic of a creature long gone. 'Thank you, Mama,' she said dully.

'Yes, well,' her mother said. She added, her tone distracted, 'And your father will see to it that de Bougainville is well and truly dealt with.'

'What? Surely he's not going to challenge him?'

'It won't come to that. But when he surprises the two of them—'

'But can't he forbid Henrietta to go?' Beth was on her feet.

'Henrietta's been rescued from social disgrace before—and then it meant that we had to consent to her marrying a jumped-up clerk when she could have had … And did she learn a thing? No. No, this time, she's the one who will bear the disgrace, not the family.'

'But if it should end in a duel … Papa's reputation—?'

'I told you, it won't come to that. I know these French types, all romance in the moonlight and nowhere to be seen in the light of day. And even if your father's actions were to become known, it is the fully justified response of a gentleman to the reprehensible incursion of a scoundrel.'

Beth could see that her mother's mind was made up. Then another thought struck her. 'But what about the political consequences?'

However, her mother had gone.

The day stretched out, long and tedious. Beth sat by the window in her hotel room, her book unread on her lap, and watched the street below. *I've done all that I can.* Then she worried over the events once more, only to come to the same conclusion again and again. The governor wouldn't be pleased if her father were to come into conflict with a high-ranking officer on an expedition backed by the French government. She had thought to prevent a scandal but she had been instrumental in creating an even bigger one.

If Henrietta followed her plan to leave while Rose and her mother were at Carter Lodge with Mrs Wood, then she'd be leaving soon. Beth knew she had to catch her before she left. She stepped quickly out into the corridor. When she reached Henrietta's door, it was ajar. She entered to find Susan was there, picking up the piles of dresses and shawls that lay strewn about the bed and chairs. Henrietta must have had difficulty choosing her attire for her assignation.

'She's gone, Miss Beth,' Susan said. 'Off to join the others at Carter Lodge. Will you be visiting them too, Miss Beth? I need to tell the kitchen.'

'No, not me, I'll be dining here with Papa. Though, I don't know about Papa. You'll need to ask.'

Beth returned to her room. She paced the floor, too agitated to sit. The Turkish carpet was not a fine one of its kind, chosen as it was to withstand wear from the feet of many hotel guests, but it had an intricate pattern that repeated regularly around its borders. Beth began to place one foot into each square as she stepped. Soon she was breathing steadily in time with each footfall. As she regained control, the realisation came to her as to what she needed to do.

Write to Baron de Bougainville.

She didn't know if the baron would be familiar with Henrietta's writing—perhaps they had already exchanged billets-doux—but she knew Henrietta's penmanship well from her letters sent from Calcutta. Sporadic as they had been, she'd treasured those letters, re-reading them for the sheer pleasure of hearing from her exotic sister who'd disappeared from her life so long ago. She'd even practised Henrietta's hand when she was young, trying to create a signature that conveyed a personality far richer than her own.

She applied herself to the task.

On her first attempt at pretending to be Henrietta, she warned de Bougainville that her father was coming to fight him and pleaded with him not to come. She put down her pen, re-reading the words. No, it wouldn't do. A military man such as the baron wouldn't back away from such a fight—to do that would be cowardly, particularly since Mr Burbridge was older, shorter and far less fit for such an encounter. Even if she wrote to him as herself and not pretending to be Henrietta, this would be his reaction.

She tried again. This time, she wrote begging for his forgiveness but saying that she had to break the liaison because of her duty to her family and her love of her children. She got as far as sealing this letter so that it could be sent, before realising that any man as passionate as de Bougainville—the image of the two entwined lovers swam before her eyes—well, such pleas would melt him. He'd promise eternal love and devotion rather than withdraw his attentions.

She thought of Henrietta—how would Henrietta go about excusing herself from a commitment that she no longer wished to keep? She had it. Beth wrote that another engagement, which she had quite forgotten, had arisen that prevented her from meeting with him as arranged. She did hope that the few days remaining of his visit to Sydney would be enjoyable and she wished him a safe journey home.

It was a short letter, but Beth thought that even Henrietta would have been proud of its subtlety. Before she could have any further thoughts on the matter, she took it to the hotel clerk with instructions that it be hand-delivered as a matter of urgency to Commodore de Bougainville on board his vessel.

Chapter 11

Everything ready for Henrietta

Two years later

Beth stood on the verandah, trying to prepare herself for the day ahead. It was the threshold of dawn, the night bird noises hung in suspension and the frogs and crickets had abandoned all hopes of love.

It is all my fault. It was two years since Henrietta had left Sydney so hurriedly, but Beth still woke in the morning darkness, jolted into the day by the consequences of her betrayal of her sister. In the immediate aftermath, Richeley, thunderous with rage, forced Henrietta to leave for Calcutta with him, leaving their children behind.

Why didn't I leave things alone? If she had done nothing, then Henrietta and de Bougainville's assignation would have occurred, but the affair would have remained secret. Beth was the one who exposed the plan and so she must bear the consequences. Since that time, her mother ignored her, and the only thing that occupied Mr Burbridge's attention was the completion of the new villa. Even Bill, on one of his infrequent visits from their Hunter property, had begun to worry about their father.

'It's all very well,' she'd heard him say to Griffith one evening, 'but what about the rest of the estate? Old

Ridgeway is complaining that he can't get Father to even visit the saltworks.'

Griffith had added his own complaints. 'I can't see how he expects to see a return on the seal trade if he's not prepared to put up the same stake as Simeon Lord. The partnership won't hold without further investment. And then I'll be left as captain of a ship that carries naught but barnacles.'

Even Rose was lost to her. As the months had passed, Rose had picked at the scars on her heart until they festered. Henrietta was to blame, of course, but Beth was a collaborator. After all, as Rose accused— how else did Beth come to know of Henrietta's assignation with de Bougainville?

And now, finally, I have to face Henrietta. Only the day before, the news had arrived that Henrietta was on a ship due into harbour. The message made no mention of Mr Richeley, nor did it provide any explanation or information as to how long she was to stay.

Beth wrested herself from her ruminations and went inside. In the drawing room, she leafed through the pile of music sheets, peering at the titles in the light of her lantern for Henrietta's favourites. She selected three pieces by Pleyel and placed them on the piano. The others she put back on the shelf. She stepped about the room, pausing every so often to scrutinise the scene. She replaced the bookmark between the pages of Coleridge's *Poetical Works* and placed the book, shut, on the side table. She consigned a decorative fan to a drawer, replacing it with an ornate music box. She paused at the door for one last look, then nodded in satisfaction.

By the time the lantern's gleam could be seen in the upstairs window, the sky had greyed. In the distance, the dawn derision of the kookaburras echoed.

The door creaked faintly as she slid into the bedroom.

'Everything ready for Henrietta, then?' Rose's eyes were open, her tone hard and weary from the sleepless night.

'Yes,' Beth whispered. In truth, she wasn't sure.

Light rain fell all morning, and the slate-grey of the harbour mirrored the dull sky above. The damp kept the Burbridges in the carriage as they waited for the passengers and their belongings to be unloaded.

Griffith alone paced the wharf, the collar of his greatcoat pulled up about his ears as he veered around the barrows trundling past. 'Oi, over here!' Griffith abandoned any vestige of gentlemanly veneer and ran towards Henrietta, where she stood surrounded by packages, trunks and assorted baggage. From some of the crates poked the fronds of exotic ferns and, under the rough cover of a tarpaulin, Beth could see the legs of what appeared to be a small pianoforte.

Henrietta turned at his shout and he enveloped her in a bear hug. Mrs Burbridge and Rose climbed down out from the carriage and, fighting her wish to stay curled in her corner, Beth followed them. Henrietta looked around, as if searching for sight of her children and, recognising their absence, her smile faded.

Activity broke out while Mr Burbridge gave instructions for Jack to get lively and sort out the baggage. Mrs Burbridge stood scrutinising the pianoforte, her brow furrowed.

Then Beth noticed that an Indian woman, her face and body shrouded in her muslin sari, stood a short way from Henrietta.

'Is she yours, Henrietta?' Mrs Burbridge didn't lower her voice.

Henrietta sounded unconcerned. 'She's Lakshmi, the ayah, Mama. You had one when you lived in India, didn't you? I'm sure I remember you telling us all about it.'

'It's out of the question. You can't keep her. Why didn't you bring Sarah back with you?'

Henrietta's eyebrows arched, but her tone remained calm. 'Oh, Sarah got it into her head to see England. So as one of my Calcutta acquaintances was going home, she kindly agreed to take Sarah on as her maidservant. But Lakshmi here was my own ayah when I first went to Calcutta. I don't know what I would have done without her. And I certainly didn't want to come back to Aylesford again without contributing something to the household. I know how you're always complaining about getting good servants—'

Mrs Burbridge took Henrietta by the elbow so that they turned away from the group to continue their conversation. 'And are you to bear the cost of her upkeep?'

'Well, of course, if you think I must. Though she doesn't cost much at all. I'm sure your own servants here cost much more. It would be a saving really, rather than taking on additional staff.'

'Our servants are paid for through the convict assignment, as I'm sure you must be aware. Look at her, Henrietta. She won't do. And I do remember them. They're filthy, Henrietta. Bare feet in the house, no idea of basic sanitation. No, it won't do at all.'

The pause lengthened between the women.

Mrs Burbridge added, 'And Tyler may help you dress your hair.'

Mrs Burbridge and Henrietta's eyes were locked. Beth thought of the staring game she and Rose played when they were children. She wondered who would blink first.

'Yes, of course, Mama.' Henrietta leaned forward and kissed her mother's cheek. Then she turned, and this time it was she who steered her mother by the elbow back towards their father. Henrietta's smiled flashed and, seemingly forgetting his anger, Mr Burbridge's face lit up in return. 'Papa, it is so generous of you.' Henrietta said. 'Mama has told me that I will not need my own servant at all, as you will be providing for all such things during my visit.'

Mr Burbridge's eyes returned to steel.

Chapter 12

We received news

Beth did all she could to stay away from the house in the weeks that followed. While Henrietta had agreed to let the children continue their schooling with the Wilkinsons, she insisted that they return to live with her.

After a longer ride than usual, by the time Beth had seen that Star was taken care of and safely grazing in the small paddock with her sisters' horses, it was fully dark. Only the shaft of light from the back verandah guided her steps back into the house.

It was oddly quiet, and she was struck by the absurd thought that everyone had left: her parents, sisters, even the servants. She couldn't even hear Henrietta's children—the constant thumps and shouts of Alec and Artie strangely absent. Her footsteps echoed on the polished floorboards as she walked down the hallway. 'Rose?' she called softly.

Instantly, Rose appeared, stepping out into the hall from the drawing room. She clasped Beth's hands. 'Poor Henrietta,' she said, her voice low and tremulous.

If the silence was disquieting, Rose's sympathy for Henrietta was even more so.

'It's Mr Richeley. He's, he's dead, Beth.' Rose drew her into the room.

Henrietta sat on the settee, unmoving, her back straight. Her head was bent pieta-like over her children. Eliza was seated beside her, her arms encircling her mother's waist. The two boys were kneeling with their heads in her lap and their arms about each other's shoulders. The tableau was painted in the dim light of a single lamp.

Out of the shadows of the room, Mrs Burbridge was the first to break the silent stillness. 'But why have we only come to hear of this now? You say he died eighteen months ago?'

Henrietta nodded her head mutely.

Mr Burbridge, who had been pacing the room, stopped, peering again at the letter. 'If we could have some more light in the room, then perhaps I can tell you.' His voice was harsh, his features set.

'Beth, do get Susan to see to it, if you would,' said Mrs Burbridge.

Beth almost ran the length of the hall to find Susan. She couldn't understand what had happened. Mr Richeley dead. And dead for near on two years. Surely then, Henrietta must have known when she first arrived? Beth cast her mind back, raking her memories. Henrietta's face did harden when she talked of Mr Richeley, but Beth had taken that to be the way of long-married couples, to affect a kind of weariness with each other.

She found Susan busy doing the family's darning by the light of the kitchen fire. 'Susan, lamps are needed for the drawing room.' Beth hung back, letting Susan go before her.

When she stepped back into the room, it was brilliantly lit. The little tableau had been shattered.

'I'll be up to see you in a minute,' Henrietta whispered as she hugged the boys. 'Eliza, can you see to them?'

Eliza was crying, silent tears washing her cheeks.

Henrietta's eyes were dry.

Mr Burbridge was re-reading the letter in his hand.

'So, when did he die?' asked Mrs Burbridge. Her words were sharp and unmodulated by any thought for her daughter's feelings, but Henrietta didn't even wince.

'The letter says it was two weeks after—' started Henrietta.

'Two weeks after the *William Young* sailed from Calcutta,' Mr Burbridge said.

'But you were with Mr Richeley before he sailed for London?' Mrs Burbridge was relentless.

'No. He had to flee to the other side of the Maharatta Ditch so as to be outside the reach of the courts.'

'And why, pray, was that necessary?' asked Mr Burbridge.

'We received news from the pilot at Sand Head that the agency was—'

'Bankrupt?'

'Yes,' she whispered.

'But you were not by his side?' Mr Burbridge asked after a moment.

Henrietta looked pleadingly at her mother.

'She couldn't live in Black Calcutta,' explained Mrs Burbridge. 'It's certainly not a place for a respectable white woman. But why didn't you join him to go to London? Piggott, Davidson and Robertson are a large firm, and surely they will regroup and—'

'They *were* a large firm,' retorted Henrietta, showing the first signs of coming back to herself, 'and it was Piggott, Davidson, Robertson … and Richeley.' She joined her father where he was standing by the fire. Facing him she said, 'And the dates are easily explained. Look again at the captain's letter. He says Richeley took ill and died just two weeks out from Calcutta. But the letter wasn't written until the ship arrived in London. And then, even if the letter was sent soon after it was dated, it took another six months to cross the world once more.' Henrietta turned to leave. 'And truth be told, the dates are unimportant. I need to be with my children.'

'But still, why not go with him?' asked Mrs Burbridge.

But Henrietta was already out of the door.

The silence Henrietta left behind was palpable.

Mr Burbridge crumpled the captain's letter in his fist and let it fall.

Beth stared at it, lying in the centre of the rug and longed to pick it up. She smoothed the folds of her dress, as if they were the sheets of paper—she could feel the creases running beneath her fingertips.

'Your father and I need to talk alone,' Mrs Burbridge said.

Beth tapped quietly at Henrietta's door. If Henrietta didn't want to be disturbed, then the knock was soft enough to ignore.

The door opened almost immediately. Henrietta's children lay curled together on her bed, their sleeping faces angelic in the candlelight.

'Are you all right?' Beth felt the banality of her words, but she had no others.

Henrietta shrugged. She was in her nightgown, her shawl draped about her shoulders. Her hair lay in rough swirls about her shoulders, let down but unbrushed. Henrietta drew her inside. 'Sit with me a while?' she asked softly.

They sat in the window seat, Beth upright, Henrietta folded in on herself, a cushion held tight to her chest.

'Did I ever tell you about the trip we took up the Hugli River?' Henrietta said. 'It was our wedding tour, but it only lasted two weeks. Richeley insisted we had to get back to the business. Uncle Piggott had made him a partner, and he was so determined to be a success.' Her eyes grew unfocused as she remembered. 'I had no idea what to expect—I was so young, barely sixteen. But it was …' She fell silent again, and Beth shifted uncomfortably.

'Does it make a difference, now that he's …?' Beth regretted the words the moment she'd begun. What she'd meant was that Henrietta had always seemed so separate from her marriage, so independent —surely life would be much the same now.

'Of course it does.' Henrietta's voice rose slightly, and Eliza stirred in her sleep. 'Of course it does,' she repeated more quietly. 'A widow.' She shuddered. 'You know in India they burn widows. Sati, they call it. Oh, it's meant to be illegal, but it still happens. I saw one once. It was when I was compelled to stay in Calcutta after sending poor little Eliza off to Sydney. I was too far along in my confinement with Alec to go with her, of course, and Artie was sick too. I don't know how I would have managed without Lakshmi. She tried to stop me looking at what was happening, of course. I was staying in the apartments that Uncle Piggott had built above his *godown* in Shibpur, and the pyres were always burning along that side of the river. I thought it was just another funeral at first, but then the banging and chanting began and I saw her. I knew her, you see. Amrita. I'd been to her wedding. Her husband had been taken by a crocodile. She was so young. The women bore her first to the river and she removed her bracelets, then her rings and, finally, still covered by her shawl, she slipped off her necklaces. She stood, irresolute. Two of the women grasped each of her arms and thrust her into the river. Her shawl ballooned about her as she submerged. She unwound her sari and it drifted across the surface of the rippling water into a long ribbon. She let it go. She stood then, clad in a simple white shift, which clung to her form, wet and dripping. She turned to face the crowd.' Henrietta took a deep breath. 'The pyre was a raised framework of bamboo filled with logs of sandalwood and perfumed oils of different kinds. There were three tall slender pillars of bamboo on each side with rope attached to the top of each, to draw down if required at the last moment to prevent her escape. They led her to the pyre and, in an instant, flames burst forth. The crowd shouted wildly, and there was bedlam as the tom toms, brass trumpets, cymbals and gongs deafened me.'

Beth found she was holding her breath.

'Thick smoke shut out from view whatever may have passed in the last struggles.' There were tears in Henrietta's eyes as she continued, 'I keep remembering the words that Richeley translated for me from her marriage ceremony. The husband says to his bride, "I am the strength but you are the beauty; I am the fire and you are the fuel".'

The candle guttered as it neared its end.

'You know, it seems strange. I didn't think I'd be this sad.'

Chapter 13

Beth shivered as the breeze picked up

Eight years later

The mist had settled along the length of the Parramatta River, seeping here and there in noiseless tendrils among the low scrubby shores. The new villa was higher up the slope and its elevation opened the expanse below. Beth could stand on this verandah forever and still see things she had missed previously. In the early morning light, her burden of guilt eased. She could hold it at a distance and let her mind skim over old ground without becoming mired.

Eight years after her return, Henrietta spent most of her day visiting the workers' cottages on the estate. Rose suggested that it was simply an excuse for Henrietta to ride, but Beth thought her sister sought a cure for her restlessness through physicking others. Even though the new villa was larger, it was barely able to accommodate the Burbridges as well as Henrietta and her children. However, the move had meant that they'd all begun to feel settled at last and, recently, Rose had begun to return to some degree of sociability. Though, perhaps the arrival of the gentleman naturalist, Baron von Hügel, had something to do with that.

Beth shivered as the breeze picked up, and she retreated from the verandah. Griffith and Henrietta had said they would be arriving with their mysterious visitor later in the morning, and so she turned her mind to the preparations yet to be made.

Beth thought at first that the man was a servant because of his old-fashioned pantaloons and brocaded waistcoat. But Griffith and Henrietta were laughing warmly and a joke was exchanged between them, so Beth presumed the man was the promised visitor.

Griffith shepherded the stranger up to where Mr Burbridge stood rigidly by the fireplace.

'Father, I think you haven't had an opportunity to meet your nephew, so,' Griffith said, taking a deep breath, 'may I introduce you to Mr Arthur Piggott.' With no immediate response coming from their father, Griffith turned in obvious desperation to his mother. 'Mama, Mr Piggott.' And quickly, before she even had a chance to respond, Griffith swung his attention to his sisters. 'Rose, Beth, meet our cousin Arthur.'

'Pleased, I'm sure,' Beth said quickly, her eyes downcast, uncertain as to whether their parents were, in fact, deliberately snubbing Mr Piggott.

Henrietta stepped in. 'Poor Arthur kept slaving away writing letters to you after Aunt Piggott followed dear Uncle Piggott to his Maker. I told him how bad the mail boats are from India; as you know, hardly any of my letters ever seemed to reach you. So, I wrote to him to come and speak to you in person. I told him he'd be sure of a welcome.' Her voice was light and airy, almost tinkling with delight at the discomfort of her parents.

Her scorn jolted Mrs Burbridge into awareness. 'Of course, of course.' Her voice took on the dulcet tones of the society matron. 'My, my, another nephew. I have so many that it's no wonder I have lost track of a few. You are most welcome, Mr Piggott.'

Mr Piggott had kept his arm outstretched throughout all of this, as if waiting for Mr Burbridge to shake his hand. He was in his mid-thirties, but his round face reddened in a way that didn't bode well for his complexion in later life.

Mr Burbridge muttered, 'Well, family's always welcome, I'm sure.'

Mr Piggott dropped his arm, clearly recognising that this was as much a greeting as was going to be forthcoming.

Griffith was shifting uncomfortably from one foot to the other. He gave Arthur a would-be jovial clap on the shoulder. 'Well, I for one am glad to see you in this half of the world, Piggott. This time I'll be the one showing you about the traps. I owe you some sightseeing after all the places you took me around in Calcutta.'

Mr Piggott gave a forced smile. 'I'm embarrassed to think how I boasted about the delights of the Hugli River, now that I've seen this harbour of yours. I always thought you were exaggerating, but you weren't.'

Introductions over, Mr Burbridge abruptly excused himself and headed to the library, immediately followed by his wife.

After a dismissive shrug, Henrietta said, 'Out with it, Griffith. I can see that you are desperate to tell us something.'

'I really shouldn't say.' Griffith fought down a grin.

'Beth will tell me, won't you Beth.'

'Oh, she doesn't know.' Griffith checked the door. 'All right. I haven't told Papa yet, so this goes no further than us.'

Mr Piggott looked intrigued. Henrietta waited.

'Miss Wood, Mary, and I, well,' he said, stumbling over the words, 'we're engaged to be married.'

'Of course,' cried Henrietta. 'I knew it. You've kept her waiting long enough.'

'Papa won't be pleased,' Rose said.

'Why on earth not?' Henrietta said. 'She's from a respectable family; her father's a judge. And Griffith is the perfect age for a man to marry—'

'Mr Justice Wood's family background is Irish,' Rose added.

'But not Catholic,' Griffith hastened to clarify. 'And Giles Wood was raised and educated in London. It's more that he's a bit Whiggish in his political leanings.'

'Oh!' Henrietta waved her hand in a dismissive gesture. She looked to Beth. 'What do you think?'

Beth flushed with pleasure. Henrietta usually acknowledged her only as an audience.

She chose her words carefully. 'Mrs Wood was a great friend of Mama's when they were at school together. She was so pleased when they came to Sydney. But—'

'And do Mr and Mrs Wood know?' Henrietta's eyes were glazing over.

'Mrs Wood is very pleased,' said Griffith.

'Oh, I see.' Henrietta's expression mirrored Griffith's. 'But Mr Justice Wood isn't forbidding the marriage?'

'Well, she's of age,' said Griffith. 'But no, he's not the sort of man to do that.'

Chapter 14

So little to say

Dinner parties were excruciating torment. At a picnic or a ball, Beth could fall back to the periphery, but a dinner required her to fully engage. This was particularly so if the dinner was being held by the Burbridges. As they had got older, she and Rose would be pushed forward to be admired, talked to and evaluated. With the passage of years had come responsibility for acting as a full participant in the adult conversations. It was no longer enough to smile prettily and say, 'I'm sure I don't know'. Being women, of course, their opinions and contributions were not attended to in any serious way, but still they were expected to give them, and their social worth was increasingly evaluated in that regard rather than their appearance.

The only part of such occasions that Beth enjoyed was in the lull between when all was in readiness for the guests, but before they arrived. By then she'd checked the progress in the kitchen, seen that the drawing room had been laid out with the best silver and glassware, and that Susan and Mary's fresh aprons were tied. She'd go upstairs, slip on her gown, and then help Tyler dress her mother's hair and pick out her jewellery. Her mother's features were strong and, with the lustre of the large drop pearl earrings adding a sheen to her complexion, her eyes sparkled with anticipation of the evening ahead. Even Beth could feel that something magical was waiting a little way ahead.

'Have you women stopped fussing about?' barked Mr Burbridge, the sound of his footsteps heading down the stairs.

Beth loved to see her father in his white tail coat and black trousers. He had a full head of hair and, rather than greying, it was slowly changing to a brilliant white that gave him a statesman-like quality.

Beth and her mother followed him down to the drawing room where they would be meeting their guests. Rose was already there. Her heart-shaped face was set off by her large expressive eyes and, with her hair in the latest fashionable ringlets, she could have been taken as barely twenty rather than ten more. Baron von Hügel would be coming, and Beth's stomach tightened in sympathy with her sister's nervousness.

Griffith and Bill came in, bringing with them a heady swirl of tobacco and whisky and the smell of horses that no amount of scrubbing up for the occasion could expunge. They'd been smoking cigars out on the verandah. The whisky was probably Griffith's idea, Beth thought, though Bill was no slouch where drink was concerned either.

At their father's frown, Bill protested, 'A fellow has to congratulate his little brother on embracing the ball and chain. Poor Miss Wood — to even contemplate such a feckless husband.'

Their brotherly chivvying was interrupted by the guests who all arrived together—Baron von Hügel having taken up the invitation to share the carriage with Mr Justice Wood and his daughter. Beth marvelled at the way her mother managed to create an atmosphere of conviviality, despite both fathers of the engaged couple having so little to say to one another.

When Susan came to stand by the door, Mrs Burbridge murmured quietly to her, 'Tell Mrs Holder we'll be another five minutes. We're still waiting on Mrs Richeley. Get Mary to give her a hurry along.'

'My sister still thinks she's in India,' Griffith said. 'Absolutely no point in trying to dine there until the evening cools down.'

'And how the dinners would go on,' Mrs Burbridge said, her smile a little forced. 'I can remember trying to stay awake until my parents returned from their dinner parties with Governor-General Hastings.' She then added in an aside to Baron von Hügel, 'My father was Comte Louis de Perroquet, you know. He'd been an officer of the bodyguard of King Louis XV.'

'So, he fled France?' the baron asked.

'I was so young when he died, I did not hear it from him. My mother said that the unrest when King Louis XVI came to the throne prompted him to move to India—'

Her tale was interrupted as Henrietta entered arm-in-arm with her daughter, Eliza. Having gained the attention of the room, the two of them curtsied.

'My apologies for being so tardy,' said Henrietta, 'but there's a harvest moon rising. Even this early, it's so large that we could see it hovering there, as if daring the sun to hurry up and slide below the horizon.'

While the attention was focused on Henrietta, Mr Piggott had slipped into the room. He took up a position beside Griffith, content to nod his head in response to introductions and to sip the whisky that was offered. Although Mr Piggott had been living under the same roof for the last several weeks, Beth had not found herself in anything resembling a conversation with him. While he seemed personable, he was a quiet man, and apart from several long sessions with her father, he did little else than appear for meals, and go to his room.

He didn't ride, nor did he appear to consider walking a pastime. Beth wondered whether he might be a reader, in which case perhaps he and Papa had been selecting books of interest for him from the library. However, she had not had the opportunity to find out since he spoke so little.

Although there were only twelve for dinner, they proceeded into the dining room in the formal style. Mr Burbridge led the way with a flustered Mary Wood, with Mrs Burbridge following on the arm of the baron. Mr Justice Wood took Henrietta's arm, and Rose was accompanied by their cousin, Mr Piggott. Bill took Beth's arm rather grudgingly. He detested dinner parties almost as much as she, so she wasn't offended. Henrietta's daughter was hanging back, uncertain, until Griffith tucked her arm in his and whispered something to her that made her giggle.

Their dinner was served *à la françaisse,* so the initial silence of the company was eased by the need for plates to be filled and discussed and passed about. Mrs Burbridge had seated Mr Justice Wood as far away from her husband as she could to minimise the chance of conversation of a political nature.

'I'm so pleased we were able to lure you away from your work,' she said to him. 'It is such a pity Mrs Wood isn't well enough to join us. Though, perhaps the news of the engagement might have given her some cheer?'

'She's exceedingly pleased,' Mr Wood answered. 'As are we all, of course,' he added hastily.

Mrs Burbridge's attention was distracted by the sound of raised voices coming from her husband's end of the table. The disadvantage of the seating arrangements, which Mrs Burbridge had not been able to surmount, was that Mr Piggott was seated towards her husband's end of the table. The two men's faces were flushed, but they fell silent the moment the eyes of the assembled party were upon them.

Baron von Hügel cleared his throat. 'Madame Burbridge, I must congratulate you on your fine offspring. I had not thought to find such erudition and refinement in a colony as remote as this. I am sure this achievement is all down to you.'

'Not at all, Baron, though it is most gracious of you to say so.' Mrs Burbridge inclined her head. 'The boys of course had the advantage of some fine tutors, but for the girl's education, my contribution really was borne out of necessity. It was impossible to get, let alone keep, a governess back then. No sooner had you lured them out here, that they up and married some ne'er-do-well. Why, even our master salt-maker, Mr Ridgeway—'

'You're too modest, Mama,' said Rose. 'I've been telling the baron how, every day after our lessons, you'd accompany us out rambling, encouraging us to collect and draw our little harvests, and then consider how we might categorise the ones that were unknown to us.'

'And not just unknown to you,' said the baron. 'Mr Maclean, the Assistant Superintendent at your Botanical Gardens, sings the praises of the Burbridge sisters in contributing to the collections.'

Rose's colour was high and she kept her eyes fixed on her plate.

Mrs Burbridge said, 'We are blessed with many opportunities here for those with discipline and application. Not all my children were so diligent, unfortunately.'

'No point in worrying over flowers or their Latin roots,' said Bill, his mouthful of steak barely swallowed. 'All I need to know is what the cattle will eat and what they won't.'

'While the stock you bring down to the yards keep being as fat as the ones you brought last year, I'm not about to quibble about your Latin,' Mr Burbridge said.

'But discipline is the key,' continued Mrs Burbridge, looking at Henrietta. 'Boys run wild without a firm hand.'

'Oh, Alec and Artie share their father's high spirits,' said Henrietta. 'All we need to do is get them their own ponies and they'll be out from underfoot from dawn to dusk.'

'Can I interest you in the peas?' Griffith passed the bowl to Mary Wood, who was sitting on his left.

'Would you be thinking of doing anything more than just looking at the plants while you're here?' asked Bill. 'There's some land up our way in the Hunter that would make a sound investment. It's overridden with blacks of course, but I'm friendly with a couple of them. I'm sure we could convince them to move on with the right inducements.'

'Are the natives a problem in the Hunter?' asked Mr Piggott.

'If a visitor may be forgiven for making an observation,' said the baron. 'It would be most unfortunate if the Hunter were to adopt the process that I was told about when we stopped in Van Diemen's Land. Proclamations of land boundaries will mean nothing, and enforcement will only add to their suffering.'

Bill took a large swig of his claret before replying. 'When you come up our way, you might want to keep your observations to yourself—visitor or no.'

'The Aborigine people are very knowledgeable about plants, I find,' Rose hastened to say. 'One of the women who helps with the laundry, old Becky, she's been able to tell me—'

And the evening limped on.

Normally, Mr Burbridge would stand to signal that it was time for the men to retire from the table for cigars and port, but he seemed reluctant to move. Perhaps it was the thought of being in the company of both Mr Justice Wood and Mr Piggott without the mediating skills of his wife that was fixing him to his seat.

Eventually, at Henrietta's suggestion, they all went out to a section of the verandah that she had arranged to net with some of the muslin mosquito netting that she'd brought back from India.

'This time of evening is the best, I think,' Henrietta said. 'The air feels as soft as velvet but, as mosquitoes and every other insect agree with me, we rarely get to enjoy it.'

'Rose, why don't you take one of the lanterns and show the baron those native hyacinths we came across the other day?' suggested Mrs Burbridge.

The baron, looking relieved to escape the hostility still emanating from Bill, followed Rose with alacrity.

As Beth watched them go, she wondered if she should feel envious. Baron von Hügel's aquiline features radiated intelligence. He spoke kindly to her, but his notice was reserved mainly for Rose. Rose had told her of his romantic history at length. The baron had been childhood sweethearts with a Hungarian countess, only for her to reject him and marry royalty instead—Prince Metternich. And, worst of all, the Prince had been one of the baron's closest friends. So, with a broken heart, the baron had been wandering the world for the last three years. The pain of romance was the stuff of the novels she liked to read, but why would she envy her sister when Rose spent each day in a turmoil, sometimes elated and sometimes in moody contemplation?

At Mrs Burbridge's suggestion, the men lit pipes and cigars. The atmosphere eased into sporadic conversation and comfortable silences.

'And did you bring back any other fabrics with you from India, Mrs Richeley?' asked Mary.

Henrietta's reply was cut off by Mrs Burbridge.

'They make such extraordinarily fine silks there, I quite expected to see your shawls, Henrietta.' She fingered her own shawl about her neck. It was of the deepest crimson, the silk weave ornately embroidered.

'And is your shawl from India too, Mrs Burbridge?' Mary asked.

Griffith beamed at his fiancée for her conversational compliance.

'Yes, I've had it since I was five years old. When I was leaving India, the governor-general's wife, Mrs Hastings, wrapped it about me and, pressing a purse of sixty gold mohurs in my hands, insisted that they were for me to buy toys for my voyage.'

'You were so young. Do you remember the journey? You must have had such an adventure.'

'No, perhaps it all was too long ago.'

If Mrs Burbridge was seeking to extract a compliment about her age, Mary missed the opportunity.

'My last trip back from India brought me the most astonishing experience I think I have ever had,' Henrietta said. 'Have you ever heard of the Zoroastrians?'

'Some Indian superstitious nonsense or other,' said Griffith by way of explanation.

Henrietta ignored him. 'Our ship's cook was an adherent and he insisted on keeping a flame alight at all times, night or day. Time and again, the captain ordered him to desist, but he wouldn't. One night, a fire started in the galley.'

She had their full attention.

'An investigation revealed that the cook had fastened a candle to the mast where it ran down through the galley. By the time they found it and extinguished the blaze, the mast was charred and barely sound.'

'What did they do to the cook?' Mary asked.

'Lashed him within an inch of his life,' suggested Bill.

'Yes,' said Henrietta. 'But no amount of whipping could make him repent. The captain ordered that he be taken to the brig, but he broke free. He leapt over the rail and into the sea below, shouting words I didn't understand.'

'Did they save him?' asked Mary.

'Should have left the blighter to drown,' said Bill.

'The captain ordered the men to lower one of the boats, and so they rowed after him. Each time they came close, he swam away, still shouting something in his own language.' She sighed. 'Eventually, as the sun was setting, they gave up. By the time they returned, his head had disappeared beneath the waves.'

Beth sank deep into the cushions of the cane lounge and watched as Henrietta sparkled, her hold secured as the centre of attention. Griffith and Mary laughed easily at the slightest witticism, so far in love that everything around them was touched by their happiness. Even Mr Piggott chimed in where he could, and Mr Justice Wood looked on, beaming at his daughter's happiness.

Mr Burbridge and Bill had been talking about matters on the estate, but they fell silent. Perhaps feeling an obligation as a guest to at least say something to his host and future relation by marriage, Mr Justice Wood directed his attention to Mr Burbridge.

'So, what do you think of the news from India, Mr Burbridge?'

'What? What's that?'

'I don't know much about it,' Mr Justice Wood replied, 'not being a businessman, myself, you understand. But I see a couple of bankruptcy cases have come onto our court lists from local agencies who mainly depend on the British East India Company trade.'

Mr Piggott exchanged a look with Henrietta. Her lips tightened.

Mr Burbridge blustered his way through a response. 'I thought they'd ironed out the problems they had following the new Charter. We weathered the changes after the Charter of 1813, there's no reason why the new Charter of 1833 should be any different. In fact, Griffith seems to have done all right out of it from the amount he spends. Canton's coping with it all, isn't it, Griffith?'

Clearly discomforted, Griffith tried to deflect. 'Oh, Piggott here knows more about all that sort of thing than me.'

Mr Justice Wood took in the panicked looks of some among the party. 'The agencies have been struggling a good while, I understand.'

'So, what's the situation then, Piggott?' Mr Burbridge leaned forward. 'I thought you said one of your father's partners—Davidson, wasn't it—had

shored up a deal with that lot in Canton to refloat the
agency?'

After a quick apologetic glance at Henrietta, Mr
Piggott replied, 'When I left—' He broke off, before
continuing, 'In fact, that's why I'm here. We need to call
in every outstanding debt owed to us. Essential to
avoid personal insolvency.' He nodded to Mr Justice
Wood.

Mr Burbridge rose to his feet. 'Essential, be
damned.'

Chapter 15

It's you that this matter concerns

Beth perched on the edge of the hard-backed chair stationed outside her father's library. Her shoulders ached. She longed to slump, as she'd seen Henrietta doing when no company was present. But she feared that her mother or father would emerge to tell her to come in at any moment.

She trawled through the events of the dinner party. Initially, she'd welcomed the novel suggestion from Henrietta of the verandah, as it had allowed her to recede from the company, to watch and, in so far as she could when others were present, to relax. But when the conversation had turned sour, she hadn't been paying much attention.

She had been watching the dimly visible figures of Baron von Hügel and Rose wandering about the garden. It wasn't until her father's sudden leap to his feet that she'd been brought back to alertness. She'd feared there'd be shouting, but her father recollected himself, his neck bulging in the effort to fight back whatever it was that he wanted to say next. He'd bowed stiffly and gone back inside.

His words had hung in the air, as large as the orange harvest moon hanging above the trees. There'd been a long silence, during which Henrietta and Mr Piggott seemed to be attempting to converse by telepathy — their mutual gaze was so intense.

'Griffith,' Henrietta had said with a roguish air, 'the moon is very fetching tonight. Perhaps you and Mary should help Rose entertain the baron.'

'A good moon to light our drive back home, I think,' Mr Justice Wood had said, extricating Mary and himself from the prickly atmosphere. 'And we promised the baron a ride back too.'

The final farewells were interminable to Beth. First there had been the farewells upon rising, followed by the flurry of thanks, and then the sudden outbreak of conversation by the door while waiting for the carriage to be brought up, and then it had been another round of gratitude and compliments before the visitors finally departed.

'Mr Piggott,' Mrs Burbridge had said as the noise of the wheels had died away. 'Would you care to join Mr Burbridge and myself in the library?' The words had been polite but the tone had been icy.

Mr Piggott, who'd been finding his too-tight shoes a source of focused contemplation ever since Mr Burbridge had stalked away, seemed to shrink in on himself. His shoulders had dropped, his waistcoat buttons had strained a little more as his podge of a belly had been displaced outward.

Bill and Griffith had returned to the back verandah, and Henrietta had shepherded a sleepy Eliza towards the stairs after Rose.

Beth had suddenly become more awake than she'd been all night. Her mind churned. She could guess that some business matter lay behind whatever it was that was going on between her father and Mr Piggott. Part of her had wanted to go up to Rose and ask her about the baron, what he'd said, what she'd said. But as soon as the baron had gone, Rose's animated liveliness had disappeared. Her face had become inscrutable again. Rose wasn't going to talk about it.

Beth had made her way into the drawing room. The servants had already been in to clear away, but things were out of place, as always. Visitors would leaf through the music by the pianoforte or examine the delicate ivory carvings from China, never returning them to their original position. She'd begun to move through her routine, shifting and nudging everything back to where it should be, and her breathing calmed.

Her mother had appeared at the doorway.

'Since you're up, Beth, I'd like a word, after Mr Piggott has retired, that is.'

So here she sat, waiting, trying to think what her father would say. *Economies,* she thought. *I'll go through the accounts.* Or would it be worse than that? She was a burden on the household, she knew. *I'll be a governess.* She pictured herself, surrounded by loving children.

After Mr Piggott emerged, Beth could hear the low grumble of her father's voice, peppered with exclamations from her mother coming from behind the heavy cedar panelling.

The doors opened and her mother beckoned her inside.

Her father was seated behind the massive desk that took up a large proportion of the space in the library. Behind him, the shelves displayed the family collection of books, which was much admired for its resources on farming, land use, husbandry, botany, and British history—particularly as related to Kent. Apart from that, their classical works were no different than those to be found in any other collection of the few gentlemen settlers in the colony. There were no novels. Such works of fiction they owned were to be kept in their bedrooms and out of Mr Burbridge's sight.

Mrs Burbridge was too agitated to sit. She was taking short steps this way and that. At a nod from Mr Burbridge, it was her mother who spoke first. 'You're a clever young woman, Beth, and no doubt you will have developed some inferences as to the situation that arose after dinner?'

Perhaps she wanted Beth to simply nod, and thus spare her from having to clarify further.

Beth looked from one parent to another. 'I'm really not at all sure—'

'What your mother is saying,' expounded her father, 'is that an outrageous financial situation has come upon us. Completely unwarranted, certainly not of our making.'

'Are we, are we, bankrupt?' Beth asked, her voice timorous.

'What?' her father exploded. 'Is that what you thought? Of course not, the very idea. We are as sound as the Bank of Australia, as sound as a bell.'

'It's the Piggotts, Beth,' her mother interceded. She glanced at her husband. 'Mr Piggott has come, as the executor of his father's estate, insisting that we, that is, your father, owed his father. He's claiming we owe him a very large sum indeed. But—'

'But,' interrupted Mr Burbridge, 'Piggott is the one who has debts to pay, by Jove. We're the ones who are owed. He's as much a swindler as his father was, graverobbers the lot of them. He should be ashamed. And he has the hide, the complete hide, to show his face here.' Mr Burbridge's words dried up.

Beth stared from one to the other. 'But what can I do—?'

'What, what do you mean, girl?' Mr Burbridge wheeled about. 'Aren't you part of this family?'

Speaking over him, Mrs Burbridge snapped, 'As selfish as your older sister, you're as bad as Henrietta.'

Stung, Beth tried again. 'I'm sorry, but you don't understand. What is it that I can do to help?'

At this, Mr Burbridge looked to his wife. He looked faintly embarrassed.

'It has come to our minds ...' Mrs Burbridge was clearly choosing her words carefully. 'That there is a way to put this whole messy business to rest, so that the Piggotts and the Burbridges can, well, merge their interests, as it were.'

Beth knew the way her mother's mind turned. Dread seeped through her; her clasped hands were sticky with cold perspiration. She and Rose had been subject to their mother's tactics from the moment they were out in society. She remembered Mr Babcock, who'd once been a suitor for Henrietta, then Rose, then her. She shuddered. Their mother had become increasingly desperate as the years passed without a marriage.

Her mother continued, 'Mr Piggott is a single gentleman, of good education, and—'

'And he's my *cousin*.' Beth knew that this was not an impediment, strictly speaking, but her parents had often spoken disparagingly of such matches as 'inbreeding', 'bad for the blood lines'.

'*Half-cousin*. His mother was my half-sister. Your grandmama married Mr Andrews, my father's business partner, after my father died. I've told you that story.'

Indeed, she had—many times. 'We hardly know him.' Beth's mind, initially paralysed by her mother's suggestion, was staggering back into motion. *Mr*

Piggott? Marriage? Mr Piggott evoked a faint revulsion in her, as if he might smell if she were to stand too close.

'Hardly a problem that cannot be remedied with time and propinquity.'

Beth was aware Mrs Burbridge was a strong proponent of the tenet that proximity in time and place were the sole ingredients to a suitable marriage match. To that end, she had forced Rose and Beth into endless social engagements, picnics, outings, balls and dinners, on top of regular church attendance, which intruded upon their preferred more intellectual pursuits.

'But Rose?'

This time, Mrs Burbridge paused before answering. 'I, that is we, have other plans for Rose. No, it's you that this matter concerns.'

Through this exchange, Mr Burbridge had been shaking his head as if continuing some internal argument.

Beth seized upon this. 'But, Papa,' she appealed. 'You have painted a picture of Mr Piggott's character that suggests dishonesty. He cannot be a respectable member of society—no better than a convict. Surely, you would not have a daughter—'

But she had gone too far.

The small capillaries beading Mr Burbridge's cheeks stood out as he strove to answer through his rage.

'Mr Burbridge,' cried Mrs Burbridge. 'You must sit down. Calm yourself. Here, another brandy.' And she pressed the glass into his hand. She rounded on Beth. 'Enough. How can you be so ungrateful for our solicitude for your future to suggest that we would do anything that would bring the family into disrepute.'

Beth clenched her fists, her nails digging deep into her palms. She took solace from the stabbing pressure. She spoke as calmly as she could. 'In that case, when might I expect Mr Piggott to address me on the subject?' She couldn't help the quiver in her voice.

'After he's agreed to the notion,' said Mrs Burbridge. 'I dare say it won't take him long to see the sense of it, if we approach the matter with subtlety.'

Chapter 16

You must keep a clear head in such matters

At their mother's insistence, Henrietta, Rose and Beth accompanied her to pay their respects to Mrs Wood. Beth wished she could have avoided the visit. Visiting the sick was straightforward: either the person was well enough to receive visitors or not. If not, then you could leave your card. But visiting a person who was aware they were dying left an unspoken scythe hanging in the air above the conversation, imbuing every look, every utterance with meaning and significance, however intended or otherwise.

Henrietta had agreed to the visit only after Griffith's assurance that he would be there. He had been staying in town so as to see his fiancée at every opportunity. Rose seemed indifferent. Baron von Hügel was out of town, having headed to the Blue Mountains, so there was no reason for her not to accompany their mother. Beth, who had been avoiding her parents assiduously since their discussion, consoled herself that while she was out of the house, she wouldn't have to run into her father or Mr Piggott. She would also be safe from any further importuning from her mother, since they would be in company. And besides, she reassured herself, marriage as a topic was hardly suitable for a deathbed occasion.

Mrs Wood's condition had deteriorated since Beth had last seen her. Her cheekbones stood out and her skin was waxy and grey. However, she was dressed and seated in her private sitting room to receive them. Beth thought the thin woman would have been more comfortable in bed, watching her shifting her position yet again.

'Let me sort out those cushions for you, Mama.' Mary Wood left Griffith's side to plump up the cushions behind her mother's back.

'I'll be fine, don't fuss.' Mrs Wood wore an air of resigned patience, and her eyes glowed with pride as she watched Mary retake her place beside Griffith. 'It is such a joy to see you both, sitting there like two pigeons, all billing and cooing.'

Griffith and Mary blushed in unison, and Henrietta laughed.

It was the first laughter that the room had heard during the visit thus far.

Mrs Burbridge and her daughters had adopted the long faces and reserved sympathy that was deemed appropriate for the situation. But Mrs Wood worked hard to dispel the gloom. She was all smiles and showed a febrile excitement as she went over all the plans for Griffith and Mary's wedding. The day was to be soon, far sooner than would be normally expected, but as Mrs Wood said, 'God's in a hurry, so we'd better hurry too'.

The cake was reduced to crumbs and the teapot cold by the time Mrs Wood and Mrs Burbridge had settled on all the wedding arrangements. Beth, Rose and Henrietta were required to do nought but agree that everything would be wonderful, and Griffith and Mary were not required to do anything at all.

'It's going to be lovely,' exclaimed Mrs Wood finally. 'You two run along,' she said to Griffith and Mary. 'I'm sure you'd much rather have a stroll together than be cooped up on a day like today.

In fact, the weather was overcast, oppressive with humidity, and with rain threatening from the south, where a bank of clouds was building and steadily growing darker. But, for Mrs Wood, it appeared that every day still on Earth was to be relished. Beth went to rise also, along with Henrietta and Rose, but Mrs Wood stopped them.

'No, no, I'm sure they don't need chaperones,' she said. The exertion made her cough, and it was a moment before she could go on. 'Time alone together, that's what they want. When Mr Giles Wood and I were courting ...' Her voice tailed off and a mischievous glint showed in her tired eyes. She shooed the couple out of the room with a gesture. 'And I've matters I wish to discuss,' she said looking intently at Mrs Burbridge.

Again, the three daughters made to rise.

'No, no, don't leave us. What I have to say concerns you too.' Mrs Wood smiled at Mrs Burbridge. 'Do you remember, when we were at school? And how we had it all arranged. I would marry a dashing soldier and have two boys and twice as many girls, and you would marry a rich nobleman and have—' She broke off. 'I can't remember, how many children were you going to have?'

Mrs Burbridge shook her head, smiling.

'And of course, each of my children would find their true love with yours,' Mrs Wood continued. 'And look, it came true.'

'I didn't know Mr Justice Wood had been a soldier,' said Mrs Burbridge with a twitch of her lips. 'And while Mr Burbridge comes from a family with an illustrious heritage—'

'Yes, well, not all our dreams can come true. But the thing is, that if I had a dream now, it would be that after I'm gone—'

'No, don't think that way,' Mrs Burbridge began to reply, grasping her friend's hand.

Mrs Wood's mask of frivolity fell away. 'But I must. And it's comforting to think of what's to follow. It's as if I am there with you all, in the future.'

Beth examined the lace edging of her sleeve.

Mrs Wood fought down another coughing fit before continuing, 'After I'm gone, Giles is going to need someone to look after him—someone to manage all these children.' Her expression cleared. 'I ended up having the right number, didn't I?' But then her seriousness returned. 'They think they're nearly grown, of course, but little Susannah is still only ten, after all. And Giles's work is so taxing; he can't be worrying about them too. I've told him, he must remarry as soon as possible. No worrying about what people might say. He has to think of the children.'

'They'll be fine,' Mrs Burbridge said soothingly. 'They're fine young people, all growing up so strong and intelligent, so like you both.'

At this, Mrs Wood's eyes filmed over. Her grip on Mrs Burbridge's hand tightened until her knuckles showed white. Mrs Wood's voice grew faint as she said, 'He must marry Rose.'

Rose looked up, her eyes wide. Henrietta's attention swung back to the room. With a start, Mrs Burbridge withdrew her hand.

The door flew open with a rush of wind.

'It's really starting to come down.' Griffith came in, ruffling drops of rain out of his hair. 'You'll need to get started back if you don't want to be bogged along the way.'

Mary, entering the room behind him, went immediately to her mother's side. 'Oh, Mama, you look worn out. I have been neglecting you.'

Mrs Burbridge rose, followed quickly by her daughters. 'It is entirely our fault. We have stayed too long.' She bent to kiss Mrs Wood on the cheek. 'It has been good to talk, dear friend.'

'Don't forget,' whispered Mrs Wood. 'Promise me.'

'I won't forget.' Mrs Burbridge said, giving her another kiss.

The carriage was shaken by gusts of wind, and they tied down the canvas blinds as spatters of rain were blown against the sides.

'That was unexpected,' said Henrietta.

As if they had been waiting for a signal to speak, they each began to talk simultaneously.

'I couldn't marry Mr Wood—'

'She was always a romantic—'

'Why would she—?'

'A complete romantic,' Mrs Burbridge continued. 'We were all concerned when she married him; she could have done much better. He was doing the law reports then, and Irish by background, of course. No money in the family. Nothing.'

'But educated in England?' Henrietta checked off each item on her fingers. 'And ambitious, clearly. And now a puisne judge and well salaried.'

'A list of requirements you could have done well to have thought about before you rushed into marriage yourself,' said Mrs Burbridge.

Mr and Mrs Burbridge made a point of raising Henrietta's impulsive marriage whenever Henrietta mentioned money or her lack of it, particularly if it involved any hint that she needed assistance with her or her children's expenses. As Henrietta's conversation often referred to such things, dependent as she was on her parents now, the scolding and baiting assumed a ritual quality.

Rose said slowly, 'After Griffith marries Mary, Mr Wood will be my brother's father-in-law. Marriage in such a circumstance would hardly be proper, surely? And besides, the baron—'

'Yes, I understand. But dear Rose, you must keep a clear head in such matters.' Her nod in Henrietta's direction was as if to say, *unlike your sister*. 'The baron hasn't made his feelings known.'

Rose opened her mouth as if to protest then shut it again.

'And until he does, then there's no harm in your at least entertaining the possibility that there may be other opportunities in the future. It's a lesson that all young women should take to heart.'

Rose looked from Henrietta to Beth, clearly uncertain as to which sister her mother was referring.

'She means me,' said Beth. 'She thinks that Mr Piggott may forgive the debt if—'

'But Cousin Arthur?' Henrietta's brow furrowed in consideration of the possibility.

'The Piggotts owe us, I'll have you know,' said Mrs Burbridge. 'Why, they as much as acknowledged they owed us our share of my mother's inheritance when they took you and Griffith under their wing in

Calcutta.' She shook her head. 'You should have married Mr Martin when he asked you.' Seeing Henrietta's expression, she added, 'Or at least you could have married your cousin. Growing up in the same house, I was sure that things would develop. Otherwise I wouldn't have—'

'Why can't Beth marry Mr Wood then?' cut in Rose.

'So, Rose,' said Henrietta, 'you have no concern for Beth's marriage to either of two relations, but only for such possibilities for yourself.' She tsked. 'And, to think, the poor man's wife isn't even dead yet,' she said. 'And here we are, dividing up the spoils.'

Mrs Burbridge gave her a hard stare.

Silence fell between the women. The southerly had reached them and the rain pelted against the roof of the carriage. The wind was lashing the trees, and Beth wondered if it would hail. The rain became so heavy that they wouldn't have been able to hear a word even if they'd been speaking.

Reaching Aylesford at last, Mr Chapman, sodden, clambered down from the driver's seat and opened the carriage door for them.

Mrs Burbridge edged forward, her hand out to steady herself. 'Rose, dearest, no doubt Mrs Wood simply meant to express her selfless love for her husband. I don't think we need to consider ourselves in any moral sense bound by obligation. Clearly, she is not well and perhaps is not able to recognise the import

of what she was saying. We shall say no more about it
at this time.'

Chapter 17

Why don't you see if Mr Piggott can be tempted

The Burbridge family milled about outside St James' Church in the centre of Sydney. They would have preferred St John's at Parramatta, for its convenience, but it was the Woods' choice. As members of the groom's party, they'd arrived early, not simply for protocol, but because Griffith had been driving everyone to the point of distraction back at Aylesford.

He couldn't sit still, intermittently popping his head into the drawing room to see who was ready and had come downstairs, then bounding up the stairs, two at a time, and tapping furiously on his sisters' rooms to hurry them up. His agitation meant that the Burbridges had been woken early, breakfasted hurriedly, and had travelled the fifteen miles in squashed discomfort without a break. The heat of the day was reaching its zenith, and they were parched without the prospect of relief until after the service.

'Will Mrs Wood be able to attend the ceremony, Mama?' asked Rose, opening her parasol to shade her face.

'She's insisting, I hear, and she's a determined woman.' Mrs Burbridge moved off to mingle with the other guests.

Beth guessed the reason for her sister's question. Rose's fretfulness, already at a high pitch due to her obsession with the baron, had further increased since their visit to Mrs Wood.

'Never fear, Rose. Mrs Wood will be fully occupied with Mary. She'll not be troubling you.' Henrietta smiled slyly, voicing what Beth had been thinking.

Rose narrowed her eyes. 'You're going to miss Griffith, aren't you?

'Oh, yes, of course, but I am entirely happy for him. If anyone deserves to find love, then it's Griffith, and he's found it in abundance with the Woods.'

'I dare say he won't be able to squire you about and keep you entertained once he's married.'

A flicker of a muscle at the edge of Henrietta's cheek betrayed that the shaft had hit home. 'How little you know of married life, Rose. The first few months are indeed a time when the absorption in each other is all that matters, but the time comes, all too quickly, sadly, when one longs for a wider social circle.'

Beth listened intently, standing by the corner of the building, seeking the skerrick of shade afforded by the roof overhang. The bricks radiated heat, and she felt light-headed.

'But when there is not mere attraction, but a mature meeting of the minds—' began Rose.

'There you are, Cousin Henrietta,' came a cry from behind them.

'Cousin Eliza, it has been too long.' Henrietta smiled. 'And where is your fine husband?'

'Oh, somewhere over there, talking business, I expect.' Cousin Eliza waved her hand in a bored fashion to the cluster of men in top hats on the church steps.

'My point exactly,' said Henrietta, looking at Rose. 'Tell me, Eliza, did I see Papa actually talking with Uncle Herbert over there?'

'They're being barely polite. But then, that's an improvement.'

The two cousins linked arms and walked on to the church entrance.

'Still glued together, those two.' Rose snapped her parasol down and began to follow. 'They were always like two peas in a pod, that is until Papa came back from England and quarrelled with Uncle Herbert.' She glanced at Beth. You wouldn't remember, as you were a baby, not even talking. They were always playing together, had no time for babies.'

In that instant, Beth saw the child that Rose must have been—her pretty face pinched with envy.

They filed in with the rest of the crowd, taking their orders of service from Mary's eldest brother, Edmund Wood, who was acting as steward. Griffith had taken his place by the altar, with Bill acting as his best man, standing beside him. Griffith's face was set in stone, and his hands fiddled with his cuffs.

As Beth slid into a pew next to Cousin Eliza, Henrietta slid back out and, abandoning all decorum, gave Griffith a hearty hug and whispered something to him that set him to laughing. Henrietta slid back in on the other side of Cousin Eliza.

The congregation murmured and rustled, craning their necks every so often in hopes of catching sight of the bride. There was movement and fussing at the entrance, and then Mrs Wood was carried down the side of the church towards the front and seated with her sons and daughters about her. Then Griffith's face lit up, and they all turned to follow his gaze to where Mary stood at the entrance with Mr Justice Wood, whose eyes glistened.

Mary stepped beside her father down the aisle. She was small and delicate, and her fine muslin dress accentuated her thinness.

'Not the best choice of material,' murmured Cousin Eliza.

'Tulle would have rounded her out a little more,' Henrietta murmured back.

After the ceremony, the bridal party moved to the registry, and the congregation resumed its low murmuring.

'I'd thought we might meet Baron von Hügel here. He's been visiting Aylesford a lot lately, I hear,' said Cousin Eliza. 'We have yet to have the honour of dining with him.'

'Really?' replied Henrietta, 'Uncle Herbert's planting for the vineyard might interest him.'

Rose hissed. 'Grapes are hardly to be considered native flora, Henrietta.'

Before her parents' plan, if marriage had crossed Beth's mind at all, it was to wonder how people weren't embarrassed to stand at the front of the church congregation and be lectured on the perils of physical congress outside the purpose of the procreation of children. Beth had a clear idea of what such congress entailed. She hadn't lived on a rural property that bred and raised cattle without observing such things. But the time when she had connected those observations with married people, such as her parents, it had unfortunately coincided with her mother's first attempt at matchmaking for her when she was younger. She shook away the memory of Mr Babcock's gloved hand squashing against her own.

Hearing Henrietta and Cousin Eliza gossip so companionably about husbands made Beth wonder: *Why marry at all? Is it really worth it?* Just as she'd never seriously entertained the thought of herself being married, neither had she considered the alternative of deciding to remain single.

In view of Mrs Wood's ill-health, the usual wedding breakfast had been replaced with a picnic in the Botanical Gardens on the day after the wedding. As it transpired, Mrs Wood was too unwell to join the picnic, but Griffith and Mary had spent the morning with her before joining their guests.

'Beth,' said Mrs Burbridge, 'why don't you see if Mr Piggott can be tempted with some of these lovely sugarplums?'

Beth had studiously avoided Mr Piggott for the duration of the wedding picnic so far. Without his presence, she would have almost enjoyed herself. The Woods were an easy family in their manners— naturally friendly yet not intrusive. Beside them, the Burbridges were starchy. Only Griffith really fitted in, telling stories in an attempt to top those of his new father-in-law, and then acknowledging his lack of success with good grace.

Beth had chosen a position that was in the deep shade offered by the fig tree while the rest of the party had scattered themselves closer to where the grass sloped, and it was possible to view the brilliant scintillation of the water against the white sails of the shipping traffic. Reluctantly, Beth moved out of her shady nook and offered a plate to Mr Piggott. He took it graciously enough, but he barely looked at her.

Henrietta, seated nearby, said, 'You certainly have your father's sweet tooth, Cousin Arthur. You could keep bringing Uncle Piggott plates of cakes all day until sundown and he'd still eat them.'

Cousin Arthur patted his gently rounded paunch. 'Not yet up to my father's dimensions, I think. Sadly, he also gave me his feet.' He wiggled his feet in demonstration. The leather of his shoes strained at large bunions on both toes.

'You can adopt his remedy then,' suggested Henrietta. 'I'll never forget the sight of him wandering about in his slippers when he got back from collecting us from Diamond Head.'

'And shoes slashed across the toes to accommodate the lumps and bumps,' Griffith joined in her reminiscences. 'That was Uncle Piggott, no expense spared for comfort.'

Between the three of them there was a casual warmth, and Beth waited with the plate of sugarplums for a while longer, as if she too were part of it. But their talk continued, and she handed the plate to one of the Woods' servants. As she settled herself back in the shade, she reflected that at least Mr Piggott didn't appear to have realised her parent's matrimonial schemes.

A fresh easterly was giving them a brief respite from the baking heat, and it was as though the whole of Sydney was out to enjoy the day. Friends and acquaintances mingled across the Gardens as people paid their respects to the Woods and Burbridges on the occasion of the marriage.

Mr Justice Wood wandered from one group of guests to the next, pressing them all to eat and drink, telling stories and leaving laughter in his wake. Griffith and Mary similarly moved from group to group, but all the time, Griffith kept his arm lightly about his bride's shoulders so that they were glued together, their eyes seeking each other and then smiling shyly when their gaze met.

Rose was attempting to be similarly attached to Baron von Hügel. He had been in the colony long enough to have made the acquaintance of most of the prominent people who were present and, as he talked with this person or that, Rose moved with him. However, she wasn't the only single woman to be showing an interest, and any lapse of attention on her part allowed her competitors their chance.

The Bishop's youngest daughter was in danger of creating talk as she repeatedly allowed the neck scarf that preserved her décolletage from public gaze to shift as she bent over the seated form of the baron to press more marzipan upon him. The baron seemed to enjoy the view, but clearly he had many years of experience of such flirtations. He was a wealthy man of distinction, after all, and his courtly manners meant that no woman could be unaware of his appreciation, yet at the same time they wouldn't detect any particularity in his attentions.

In fact, the more Beth watched, the less confident she was that Rose's fond hopes were well founded. He did include her in any discussion of botanical knowledge, flattering her by seeking her opinion on points of interest in the Gardens about them, but his eyes dwelt with as much interest on the plants they discussed as they did on her pretty face.

The baron's rank attracted as many of the men in the party as the women. Mr Riddell positively fawned, and Mr Campbell kept bowing obsequiously and repetitively every time the baron was passing. Beth was proud to see that her father didn't show any such obvious signs of being awed. However, he was anything but immune. If the baron was in the conversation, then Mr Burbridge's usual bombastic pomposity on every point of discussion became more considered, though no less ponderous.

'How then,' asked Baron von Hügel, 'can Britain declare itself against slavery while continuing the proliferation of such penal settlements?'

There was a general murmuring among the gentlemen who surrounded him.

'But without the convict labour, how might the colonies provide Britain with the necessary return on its investment for the costs associated with bringing them out here in the first place?' argued one of the gentlemen.

'If you want my opinion, then the Colonial Office didn't know what it had signed up for when Sir Joseph Banks and his cronies were lobbying for the settlement,' said another. 'They saw as far as the end of their noses. Get the felons out of Britain was all that mattered.'

'Costly way to do it,' came the derisory response.

'There will come a point,' said Mr Burbridge, his louder voice making itself heard, 'where the colony will need to resolve exactly this conundrum. If free settlers of any reputation,' he said, looking about him, his thumbs in his waistcoat pockets, the picture of respectability, 'are to be attracted to the colony in sufficient numbers for its continued progress, then transportation will have to cease.'

'But the cost of labour …'

All the while, Baron von Hügel remained serene, fingering his moustache while studying each face as carefully as if taking notes of some exotic plants of minor interest.

Beth, after first checking that neither of her parents was nearby, leaned back against the trunk of the tree and turned her gaze to where Henrietta strolled nearby with Mrs Ferris, the wife of the Chief Justice.

'It's amazing to see what a touch of nobility does in Sydney society,' said Henrietta.

'It was the same when we were in Newfoundland, my dear,' replied Mrs Ferris. 'And, I daresay, it will be worse still when we return home.'

Mr Justice Wood caught the remark as he joined them. 'I do hope that our good Chief Justice isn't talking retirement again? We can't do without him.'

'Well, Governor Bourke agrees with you, sadly,' said Mrs Ferris. 'All we were asking for was leave to let the poor man recover his health, but—'

'Will the governor be joining us today?' Henrietta asked.

'Things are not entirely harmonious between the judiciary and the governor,' replied Mr Justice Wood. He looked at Henrietta shrewdly. 'As I think you might well know, Mrs Richeley.'

'You have me there, I confess. I hope I never have to come before you in the dock,' she smiled.

'Beth, there you are,' said Mrs Burbridge.

Beth abruptly straightened as her mother approached.

'We can't leave your cousin without company on such a lovely occasion, can we?' Mrs Burbridge steered her in Mr Piggott's direction again.

This time, Mrs Burbridge didn't leave Beth to manage the interaction alone. Mr Piggott managed a quick smile as they approached, his gaze sliding out to the water's edge.

'The harbour is looking splendid, is it not, Mr Piggott?' Mrs Burbridge said.

'It is indeed. Though back in Scotland, we have lochs that—'

'Scotland, Mr Piggott?' Beth had thought of Mr Piggott as being from India.

Mrs Burbridge must have thought that she'd achieved her mission, for she turned away and began to chat with Bishop Broughton.

'Oh, yes, we all, that is my whole family, moved back there when my father handed over his active role in the business to the other partners.' At Beth's look of incomprehension, he added, 'Unlike some, he retained his investment. So that's why I had to go back to India as part of winding up his estate.'

Henrietta came to join them, and Mr Piggott's face immediately lit up.

'Don't let me interrupt,' Henrietta said.

'Not at all, not at all, I was telling Miss Beth …' he began, but by then Beth had made her escape.

Beth heard the two of them laughing as she wended her way through the guests. She flushed at the thought that her awkwardness might be the cause, but scolded herself with the thought that they probably hadn't even noticed her absence.

She wandered about, stopping from time to time to stand with this group or another, but she was feigning interest. At any sign that the conversation might turn to a topic to which she might have to contribute, she moved on. Eventually, she found her way back to her tree, and she leaned back grateful to be alone. She closed her eyes, listening to the sighing of the boughs above and the chatter of birds as they went about busily shredding the figs.

Then two voices singled themselves out. Two people had come to stand on the other side of the thick trunk.

'Thank goodness,' came Henrietta's voice. 'If I stay out in that sunlight any longer, Mama will insist on soaking me in lemons for a fortnight.'

'She's skilled at insistence, your mother.' It was Mr Piggott.

Beth cringed. She should move. But if she rose, then they'd see her, and she'd be expected to talk with them. Mr Piggott might not ask her to join them, but from the look on Henrietta's face earlier, she'd like nothing more than to embarrass Beth by calling her over.

'My mother, your aunt,' stressed Henrietta.

'Half-aunt.'

'Yes, well. She's no different from my half-aunt, your mother,' she said. She imitated a voice that Beth assumed must have been meant to be Mr Piggott's mother. 'If I've told you once, Henrietta, I've told you a thousand times, if you're going to ride then you'll do it side-saddle.'

Mr Piggott laughed. After a pause, he said, 'She keeps giving me this look—your mother, I mean—like she's telling me to do something. But apart from forgive their debt to my father's estate and disappear, I can't think what it is.'

'Oh that. Let's just say, she's rather taken with your status as a single gentleman.'

'What? What's that got to do with—oh.'

Beth wanted to flee but, in equal measure, she wanted to know what he would say. There was silence from the other side of the tree. She wished she could see their expressions.

'Rose is a pretty woman, to be sure,' Mr Piggott began tentatively.

'Not Rose, silly.' Henrietta's tone was mocking. 'You'll have to do better than that.'

'Oh,' said Mr Piggott again.

And in his tone, Beth heard the answer she'd feared. Her parents had spoken to her as if she had no option, but she had thought that she had something to consider, at the very least. The prospect was abhorrent, and she was sure she'd refuse—that is, if she were to be asked. But here it was. Mr Piggott's disappointment was clear.

To her chagrin, her eyes smarted. She shut them tight, her shoulders hunched, her fists clenched tight. She wouldn't behave like some young debutante who'd spent the ball sitting by the matrons near the supper table. She'd had that experience and now, as a grown woman, she wouldn't give in to such dramatics.

'Oh, no. Mr Piggott.' Henrietta's tone of voice had changed completely. 'Look.'

Beth's eyes flew open. For a wild moment, she thought they must have rounded the tree and found her.

'Perhaps it's Mrs Wood,' said Mr Piggott, and from the sound of it, he was moving away.

Beth saw that Mr Justice Wood's children were clustered about him. He was speaking to them gently and, after a brief word to Griffith and Mary, he shepherded them back up the slope to where the carriages waited.

Beth ran to join the other guests who were clustered about the newly married couple.

Holding his hand up for silence, Griffith said, 'We've had word that Mrs Wood's health has taken a sharp turn for the worse. Mr Wood has asked me to give you all his apologies for not being able to stay to farewell to you in person. But he wishes to thank you, as do we both,' he said, indicating Mary, who stood tremulous beside him, 'for sharing our celebrations.'

The couple stood together receiving the farewells from each of the guests. The atmosphere was subdued while the sadness loomed before them.

The Burbridge family regrouped and were the last people to leave, waiting for their carriage to be brought up as the shadows lengthened across the roadway.

'You know, I've often meant to ask you how that servant girl, young Sarah, turned out for those friends of yours?' Bill asked Henrietta while they waited. 'Did you ever hear how England suited her?

'I have no idea,' Henrietta replied, barely paying attention.

Beth heard Mrs Burbridge murmur to Rose as they stepped into the carriage, 'And did the baron take the opportunity to speak with you, perchance?'

Chapter 18

Today I want to ride fast and hard

The first kookaburras had barely started up before Beth could hear Henrietta's lads thumping their way down the stairs. It was Sunday, so she had to get up anyway, as did the others in the family, to attend the morning service at St John's Church in Parramatta. But she lingered, stretching under the soft sheet, which formed the sole covering needed now that summer was upon them. The sheet was one of the older ones, and she moved her bare toes across its folds, feeling the sheen slip across her skin. Her movement woke Rose, so she wrenched herself into the world, swinging her feet to the floor.

The talk at church was the same as usual.

'Rather cool for this time of year,' Mrs Broughton said.

'But so it often is,' said Mrs McPhail, 'just when we'd all like to see a bit of sunshine.'

Mr McPhail noted, 'We might see a spot of rain.'

Mr Hawkins replied, 'We certainly need it.'

The service was as dull as the conversation, and the grey sky allied itself with both. Spots of rain peppered them as they returned to the carriages for the short drive home. *Mr Hawkins will be pleased*, thought Beth.

She was out of sorts, she knew, but she couldn't shake it off. Baron von Hügel was to dine with them and it unsettled her. Sunday dinner was her day. She had always been the one to manage that everything went perfectly. The others may not notice the floral arrangements with the banksia cones and red waratahs woven together that decorated the table. But the sense of occasion would dissipate the snipes and arched eyebrows of disapproval between them for a while—at least until the custard. However, the presence of someone from outside the family changed all that. Her decorations looked shabby, like something a child might do in playing a game of tea parties.

'After I return from our excursion to New Zealand, I am greatly looking forward to our scientific meeting at the Botanical Society's rooms in the Gardens. I will be giving a paper,' von Hügel said with considerable pride. 'You would find it most interesting, Miss Burbridge.'

'Yes, indeed, of course.' Rose's cheeks were suffused with pleasure.

'And of course,' the baron continued, 'before I leave the colony, I am looking forward to being shown about the Hunter.' He nodded courteously to Bill.

'Should be an experience,' Bill replied.

Mrs Burbridge's face smiled serenely, basking in the baron's increasing attentions to Rose. 'Perhaps some music?'

'That's a delightful idea. I'd be glad to,' Henrietta said, rising to her feet.

'No, no,' said her mother, 'Rose has the far finer voice. You shall be better employed at the pianoforte. Rose, why don't you sing that piece you were practising yesterday?'

Her cheeks flushed, Rose looked at Beth, her eyes pleading. 'Come on, Beth, we can do it together,' she said, tugging Beth to her feet. Rose then gave Henrietta the music score, saying, 'You can play that, can't you Henrietta?'

'Of course,' said Henrietta. 'A simple ditty.'

The sound of Henrietta at the piano was familiar to them all, as she played—not in any dutiful sense of practising, but always with keenness, passionately even—as though she was on the high seas. What she was to play now was not of that order, of course. But she played it delicately, flirting with each note as she teased the song to join her. Beth found she didn't mind singing to Henrietta's accompaniment. It wasn't like being in the centre of the stage at all. The piano led the way for the singers who followed.

'Oh, magnificent,' cried the baron when they'd finished. 'Encore, encore.'

And so there was another song and then several more. All Beth's worries about the evening were lost in the applause.

Henrietta brought her children downstairs to join in. Artie and Alec attempted outrageous harmonies and failed, but so cheerfully that everyone clapped anyway.

As they ushered the baron outside to his carriage, Bill emerged to finalise the plans for the Hunter trip.

'You will be travelling armed, won't you,' Rose asked anxiously. 'We are hearing of more and more robberies along the road, isn't that right, Bill?'

'No need for you ladies to be concerned,' the baron replied. 'My assistant and I have experience in the military, you know. I'm sure we can protect your big brother.'

Beth thought it was good that the baron didn't catch sight of Bill's expression.

'Well, farewell,' the baron said, bowing low. 'I look forward to when next we meet.' His eyes met Rose's. 'I swear I have not heard the equal of your singing in any salon in Vienna.'

He could even be heard humming one of the tunes as his carriage pulled away from the house.

Standing with the family waving him off, it seemed to Beth that they portrayed the ideal family: the patriarch standing proud and stern; the matriarch with her arm resting affectionately around the waist of the pretty unmarried daughter; Rose aglow with the baron's praise, hopeful of his affections; the widowed daughter laughing with her nearly-grown children. And even she, at the back of the group, relaxing with the relief of the day being over, was part of the picture. For the first time on such an occasion, Beth almost didn't want it to end.

Perhaps Henrietta felt the same.

'We've been inside all day. It's still light and I feel like a ride. Anyone else?'

Her children clamoured to come, but Henrietta shook her head. 'No, don't complain. Today I want to ride fast and hard.'

'I'll come. I know what you mean,' Rose said, her voice pitched high with excitement.

Beth hesitated. 'I'll come too,' she said. 'If you like?'

Henrietta looked taken aback, then said, 'Of course.'

Beth's happiness from before deserted her.

Jack, who was usually the one deputised to bring up the horses already saddled and bridled for their rides, was attending Father Therry's service at the Catholic school in Parramatta. In his absence, they walked down to the stables and roused White, the stableman, to help with the heavy saddles. He was none too pleased to be disturbed from 'resting his eyes', having polished off an ample proportion of the dinner leftovers with other servants in the kitchen.

'It's all really too much of a bother. I don't think I'll go to the trouble of a saddle,' said Henrietta, the undercurrent of a dare in her voice. 'What do you think?'

At this, White looked more cheerful, but Beth's stomach dropped. She'd heard Rose's tales of how she and Henrietta used to ride bareback, but she'd assumed from Bill's scornful expression that the tales were designed to impress rather than necessarily truthful. Beth looked to see Rose's reaction.

'Yes, it's just the day for it.' Rose's eyes were bright and fiery.

Henrietta and Rose slipped the bridles on their horses. Rose rode Blackie, a delicate stepping mare, and Henrietta rode a temperamental gelding who had been misnamed Neddie at birth. Beth had heard White call him The Bastard when he thought no one could hear, but Henrietta had dubbed him Pegasus. He was quick and agile over rough ground, and Henrietta rode him daily. Beth insisted that White saddle up her own horse, Star, a piebald mare. Star was getting long in the tooth and was slated for the knackery, despite Beth's protests. White complied slowly with bad grace, so Henrietta and Rose were long gone before she was mounted.

She could see them on the far rise as she trotted slowly away from the house. Henrietta had let Pegasus have his head, and Rose wasn't far behind. Then they were lost to view as they entered the tall timbered bushland. When Beth reached the edge of the cleared land, she slowed Star to a halt. She drew a deep breath, inhaling the rich eucalyptus rising in the last moments of the day. The grey clouds, which had hung like a moist mask over the sky all day, broke up and shafts of gentle light filtered through the leaves. The tree trunks, their bark shed in the summer heat, shone like burnished bronze.

She was considering giving up and returning to the homestead when she heard their ringing coo-ees. They were as out of breath as their horses when they reined them in beside Beth.

'We found the old track, Beth,' said Rose.

'And don't forget the crocodile,' said Henrietta.

'The one I told you about, Beth, the path that Henrietta and I always used to take to beat Griffith and Bill to the front gates. There's an odd sort of sandstone outcrop. We always used to pretend it was the snout of a crocodile, swimming along the water. It's overgrown now. It's no wonder I could never find it. Remember, we went looking for it so many times.'

Beth remembered being dragged through brambly thickets and getting scolded for tearing her petticoats, but she had no memory of fantasy crocodiles. Watching her sisters reminiscing made her feel separate. She had no place in their memories, or their thoughts.

The last flickers of light faded from the canopy above, and the glade felt chill.

'We'd better be heading back,' Beth said.

For a while, Rose and Henrietta kept pace with her.

When they emerged onto the flatter section that served as a rough road for the cattle, Henrietta clicked her tongue. 'I'll race you.' And she was off.

Rose instantly gave chase.

Star pricked up her ears and quickened her pace, but Beth restrained her. 'Steady as you go, old girl,' she murmured. 'Let the others do what they will.'

Beth tarried on the verandah, delaying the moment she needed to enter the house. She wanted a moment to herself, to find a still point of calm. She didn't understand why her own emotions were like piano strings, resonating in sympathy with each and every pitch that was being played out between Henrietta and her parents, between Rose and Baron von Hügel, and even between her parents themselves. And then there was the constant push for her to make herself agreeable to Mr Piggott. She didn't understand her own thoughts and feelings about that, let alone the tune that her parents were playing, with her as their instrument.

She stood in the darkness of the verandah. The frogs called to each other throatily, each of their calls sounding individual notes, invisible in the clumpy grasses. A flap of wings and the low hoot of the boobook owl sounded as it swooped. One note missing in the medley.

'Forgive me, Miss Beth.'

Beth took a step back, caught by surprise. Mr Piggott had stepped around the corner of the verandah. The smell of his cigar came with him.

'I must apologise if I took you by surprise. You often seem alert to the presence of others, so I made the presumption that you realised I was here.'

'Sorry? No, no, I don't, I mean, I didn't know. Otherwise …'

It seemed an act of intimacy for him to say such things to her.

He shook his head. 'I must apologise again. My only excuse is that my own situation, as you no doubt have realised, is somewhat similarly precarious to your own.'

She was about to question him again; however, she knew with sudden clarity that it was exactly the action that her mother would wish her to take. To respond could unlock the gate that opened into the solution her mother sought.

He continued to stand there, his face in darkness, the smell of his tobacco not unpleasant in the heady mix of rising scents from the garden as the dew began to form.

Chapter 19

You're a good listener, Beth

'It's completely out of the question.'

Beth could hear her father's bellow coming from the library, even though she was two rooms away. Henrietta had been sequestered with him for what seemed like hours. Beth and her mother had heard most of Mr Burbridge's side of the conversation, as they sat sewing together, but little of Henrietta's contribution. From the fragments, Beth had gathered the gist of the argument. Henrietta's expenses had always been a sore point, and now she was asking for more. Beth's fingers slipped with sweat in the growing heat of the morning. They had to do the fine needlework early in the day at this time of year to avoid staining the delicate fabric.

'Mr Piggott has been rather less importunate of late,' her mother said, 'in relation to his insistence that your father and I owe him, that is.'

Beth realised that her mother was staring at her. She was unused to receiving such an inspection.

'His conversation with you the other night seems to have softened his approach,' Mrs Burbridge continued, a question in her voice.

Beth's breath caught in her throat.

'Don't worry,' her mother responded, 'I wouldn't stoop to eavesdropping. I chanced to see that the door to the verandah was open and realised that you were both unaccounted for.'

Beth thought back to the conversation she'd had with Mr Piggott. She wanted to argue with her mother, to reject the need for any decision at all. This matter was not of her making. But, for her, such a statement was impossible. She could no more challenge directly than she could fly.

She caught the murmur of Henrietta's voice emphasising a point, and she longed to harness some portion of Henrietta's courage. But then, even Henrietta didn't win arguments with her parents. So why then would she think that there was anything she could say or do that would alter their course? *If not Henrietta's approach, then what?* She wished she had her mother's gift for strategy so that she could outmanoeuvre her. What she needed was a way to divert her mother from the topic of Mr Piggott.

Mr Burbridge's shouted exclamations became loud enough to hear every word. 'A separate establishment? Think of the cost. You're not some tradesman's daughter. You are my responsibility now. I will not have it said that I am shirking from my duty as a father.'

Beth winced as his voice echoed down the hall. The idea that Henrietta wanted to move out of Aylesford couldn't be unexpected. Their mother spent most of every breakfast conversation detailing Henrietta's children's misdemeanours from the previous day and admonishing them in advance of the day ahead. Eliza had become so frightened of her grandmother that she startled whenever she was addressed. The boys were unperturbed, which drove Mrs Burbridge to more scolding.

Beth thought of the calm orderliness of their lives when Henrietta was absent. 'Would it be so very disgraceful, Mama, if Henrietta and her children were not living at Aylesford?' she asked.

And if Henrietta moves out, then Mr Piggott might follow her ...

'If she were an older woman.' Mrs Burbridge snipped a new length of thread and held it at arm's length before the eye of her needle. 'And even then.' She squinted, inserting the thread. 'Perhaps only if she were a far less attractive and far more pious woman.'

Beth bent to her sewing.

'As you know, Henrietta has never been one to regulate the impulse of the moment,' continued her mother. 'I am sure she has no idea how her behaviour can appear sometimes to others. I confess that all this business with the Piggotts brings back all my old worries. I am tormented by the thought of what might have happened in Calcutta. Oh, Henrietta would not think she might have done anything, anything that might be, be ... But I remember the social mores of

India.' Her tone suggested salaciousness beyond description. 'And there are so many people here who have connections with India, if any hint of impropriety were to …' She put her work down. 'I thought perhaps dear Rose might ask her, discretely of course, but …' She completed a few more stitches. 'But dearest Rose—this is such an important opportunity in her life. I really can't ask her …'

A reply was called for, but Beth was uncertain as to what, so she offered, 'Is there something you think I may help with, Mama?'

'You're a good listener, Beth,' Mrs Burbridge said as if weighing up the matter. 'And Henrietta does like to talk about what she sees as her adventures …'

Beth shook her head, not following.

Mrs Burbridge clicked her tongue in annoyance.

Beth essayed, 'So, you think she might tell me about what happened in Calcutta after—'

'After Richeley left Calcutta for England, exactly.' Mrs Burbridge looked relieved that Beth had finally grasped her concerns. 'I, of course, would never doubt the propriety of any of my children, but everyone knows of the beautiful treasures she brought back with her. Why, her pianoforte alone has drawn praise from everyone who's seen it. Even if Richeley salvaged some of their possessions from the bailiffs before he left, how did Henrietta manage to retain them during all that time she stayed on in Calcutta before finally coming back to us? Or did she somehow acquire them after he had left?'

In Beth's own ruminations on the puzzle-box that was Henrietta's life, her thoughts had never gone in this direction.

'What's all the noise?' Griffith called from the hallway.

'Griffith, whatever brings you out here?' Mrs Burbridge asked as he entered.

'Hot as blazes out there,' Griffith said, ignoring her question. 'Can't believe you two are still hard at your needlework. Though you can be grateful you're not out there in the sun.'

'We were about to finish. Tea would be just the thing, I think.'

As if on cue, Susan entered with the laden tea tray. Mrs Burbridge barely acknowledged her.

'But what's all the ruckus about?' Griffith reiterated after he'd drunk down half his cup at one gulp.

'Henrietta has vexed your father, that's all.'

'Ah, so nothing new, then,' said Griffith. 'Look, Mama, I came out to see if you'd replied to the dinner invitation yet.'

Mrs Burbridge took a judicious sip of her tea. 'Of course, your father and I would like to come to Carter Lodge to congratulate you and Mary. We would have done it well before now, but with Mrs Wood so unwell

... Well, it wouldn't have been appropriate. And besides, I've been much preoccupied with the baron.'

'Baron von Hügel?' asked Griffith, doubtfully. 'Don't tell me he has finally got around to—'

'No, no.' Mrs Burbridge cut him off sharply. 'We've hardly seen him. I had begun to think, well, never mind. Why isn't Mary with you?'

'I didn't want to tie up the good Judge's carriage for the whole day. He does have need of it himself, after all, particularly since he prefers not to ride. And besides, Mary is a bit off-colour,' he said the last with a cheerful tone, which was at odds with its content.

'Oh, are congratulations in order?' Mrs Burbridge asked.

'Calm down,' said Griffith. 'What would I know about such matters? However, she assures me that there's nothing to worry about.'

'Well, yes, then we should be hurrying up with our reply.'

'Perhaps I'll invite the baron,' said Griffith. 'Two birds with one shot, that sort of thing. Who knows, even my brother might think it a big enough occasion to warrant coming down from the nether regions.'

There was a loud bang as the library door was slammed.

'That'll be Henrietta storming off, if I know her,' said Griffith. 'I'll go and see Papa about answering the invitation.'

'I should see if she is all right,' said Beth, rising to her feet after he'd left.

'Good idea, dear …'

For a moment, Beth thought her mother was about to say 'dearest', but the word was left hanging in the air unfinished.

Beth found Henrietta by the paddock fence feeding Pegasus an apple and talking to him softly.

Beth searched for a way to begin. 'Griffith is here,' she said. 'He and Mary are having a dinner party at Carter Lodge.' She watched Star grazing quietly at the far corner of the paddock, too content with the lush grass there to come over to greet her. 'Will you ride later?' she asked, since Henrietta had not replied. 'Or perhaps it will be too hot.' She had left her bonnet inside in her hurry to follow Henrietta, and she could feel her cheeks begin to burn.

'The heat isn't the problem. I always rode when Richeley and I lived in Agra, and it can get far hotter there than here. But Mr Chapman says there have been bad storms down on the south coast and they're heading our way. I don't mind rain, but Pegasus is a complete coward if there's lightning and, I confess, even I draw the line at hail.'

'I don't know how you can ride him,' said Beth. 'Papa was going to have him put down after he threw Bill.'

'That should tell you something about Bill's riding, not Pegasus. You need to let him have his head sometimes, and then he'll return the favour. The horse I mean, not Bill.'

'That's what you want too, isn't it?' Beth blushed. 'I couldn't help hearing Father ...'

'Well, yes. It's a miserable experience living as a dependent within your family when you've tasted your own life. But then, I suppose that's not something you'd know about.'

Beth ignored the jibe. 'And you were free in India, to have your head, I mean?'

Henrietta narrowed her eyes. 'This is Mama talking, isn't it?

Beth didn't answer.

Henrietta gave Pegasus a last rub on the nose, and then with a quick pat on his rump sent him cantering away to join the other horses in the shade. 'Well, yes, I did pretty much as I pleased. Oh, you have no idea, Beth.' The words rushed out. 'Even when I arrived in Calcutta, even at fourteen, I was freer than I am here. All Aunt Piggott ever did was fuss about her babies, so I went everywhere with Uncle Piggott as he conducted his business: down to the *ghats* and *godowns*, and into the finest houses of the richest *babus* in Calcutta.'

'But married life must have been very different?' Beth was thinking more of herself if she were married to Mr Piggott.

'Things changed only for the better. We moved to Agra so that Richeley could expand the firm's business there. We had been used to having one hundred servants in Calcutta, so that's what Richeley insisted upon in our new home. There was nothing I had to trouble myself with, and we were out every evening. It's all so different there, where the civilians are at the highest levels of society. Here, it's all about the army and the governor.'

'And after Richeley left?' Beth held her breath.

Henrietta ignored her. 'Do you think dreams mean anything?'

'I never remember my dreams,' Beth said untruthfully. In her dreams, fragments of the day shattered and she fought to reassemble each piece until forced to wake before dawn to escape her failure.

'I keep dreaming about that Zoroastrian I was telling you all about. I'm on deck next to the captain, and there's the Zoroastrian, stripped to the waist, his back bleeding from the lash. He breaks free and leaps into the water. I stand watching him swim, a trail of blood from his back staining the water in his wake. And then ...' Her voice cracked hoarsely. 'I see that the man in the water is Patrick, but not as I last saw him, all red-faced and stout with too much wine, but so young, so handsome, just as he had been when we met, before he became "Mr Richeley". He lifts his arm in the air to me and shouts, "Do you think to save me? Never! My character is ruined, what have I to live for?" And he keeps on swimming. He keeps on until I can just make out the shape of his head, black against the setting sun on the horizon, and then I wake.' Henrietta drew away from the fence. Her lips tightened. 'Calcutta society has no room for the poor. If it hadn't been for Babu Dutt …' She shook her head as if to remove the memories. 'Are you thirsty? I'm really dreadfully thirsty.' She eyed the house but then began to walk away towards the Ridgeways' cottage.

Beth, unasked, followed.

When they arrived, Mrs Ridgeway greeted them warmly. She'd been Henrietta's governess, Beth knew, and she'd accompanied the family out from Kent all those years ago. She was the first governess of the great many who had quickly married and decamped, but Mr Burbridge had never forgiven her. Since she'd married his chief salt-maker, he couldn't do anything about it lest he risk that arm of his business, but her ongoing presence on the estate was one of many irritants in his life. Beth barely knew her to talk to, though of course she'd seen her often. Henrietta, on the other hand, appeared entirely at ease.

'Mr Ridgeway's put in a few bottles of the claret from Mr Herbert's vineyard, if you're interested in a taste?' Mrs Ridgeway asked, already setting out the glasses.

'Certainly,' replied Henrietta, 'though perhaps with some water, since the day is still young yet, after all. After a quick splash, she added, 'That's enough water.'

'Beth?' asked Mrs Ridgeway.

Beth was intrigued. The tension between the Burbridge brothers meant that she'd only heard of her uncle's winemaking endeavours from others outside the family, and she certainly had not had the opportunity to taste it. After her first tentative sip, she could see why Henrietta didn't want to water it down unduly. It was by far the best wine she'd tasted from the many dismal attempts that had been made.

They sat in the cool of Mrs Ridgeway's little parlour and the knot that had settled in between her shoulders loosened. She noticed a fine filigree cup on the mantelpiece and complimented Mrs Ridgeway on it.

'Oh, dear Henrietta gave it to me,' said Mrs Ridgeway with pride. 'All the way from India.'

'Well,' said Henrietta with a smile, 'not from India, as such. From Batavia. The ship stopped there on the way back.'

'And from a Prince,' Mrs Ridgeway told Beth.

Beth hadn't heard this story.

'Well, not a real prince,' Henrietta said. 'Though he was as good as a prince on that part of the island. He had amassed a huge fortune from a piece of rock out to sea that nobody else had thought to be worth tuppence.

It turned out to be riddled with bird nests, so between the trade in bird nests with China and the guano market, well he was a veritable Rothschild.'

'But what would make him give you such a valuable thing?' asked Beth.

'And there was more. I left Calcutta with nothing. Only the ayah was of value.'

Beth remembered her mother's abrupt dismissal of the Indian servant.

'The ship had to stay longer than expected in Batavia to unload the cargo, and the governor's wife undertook to offer me lodgings. It was she who introduced me to him. His house was high in the hills, surrounded by lush vegetation on all sides and with statuary dotted about. Once inside, we were presented with sweat meats and delicacies of every description, each platter carried by a different servant girl dressed in rich silk and wearing bracelets of gold. When he heard I enjoyed the piano, we were entertained with a full orchestra of every known instrument. He wouldn't hear of us leaving without bestowing upon us so many gifts that another carriage and a cart had to be arranged for us to return with it all.'

Beth could picture it all. Henrietta would have been sparkling, like she had seen her doing years before with Baron de Bougainville—all teasing and flattery. Of course, men of the world would enjoy her company. She fought back the memory of that night when she had watched Henrietta and de Bougainville from the hotel window. No, surely there was nothing more to the story with the Prince. A small thought crept into her mind and grew. *Mama is jealous—jealous of Henrietta.* Once thought, it seemed to her that she had always known it.

As they walked back to the house, clouds were massing in grey boulders along the southern horizon and the humidity was intense.

The wine somehow made Beth's steps effortless. 'Henrietta, would you mind if I asked your advice?' The words were out before she'd realised.

'As long as it is no matter of great importance,' said Henrietta, swinging her bonnet by its strings. 'Uncle Herbert's wine is far too strong for me to consider matters in earnest.'

'Mama and Papa want ... that is, they'd like to see Mr Piggott ...'

'Marry you. Yes, I know.'

Beth was all too aware that Henrietta knew. Her cheeks, alight with the heat and the wine, seared at the memory of Henrietta's conversation with Mr Piggott in the Gardens. But she persevered. 'But, I, I don't want to.'

'Oh.' Henrietta stopped short. 'Why ever not? Cousin Arthur is a perfectly agreeable gentleman. And you're not getting any younger, if I may say.'

Irritated, Beth replied, 'You like him, you could marry him, and your mourning period is well and truly over.'

'He couldn't afford me, particularly if he lets Papa get away with not paying him back.'

'But Papa could pay him easily. He's a wealthy man, even if he won't buy you every dress you want. When Uncle Piggott provided the money for the new house, he was paying back the money owed to Mama. Papa doesn't have any debt to pay. It's a matter of principle.'

'You think so? Well, I'm not going to make the same mistake twice.'

'But what if I don't want to be married, ever?'

'Ah.' Henrietta pondered. 'Not what I expected, I must say. But then marriage is not what I expected either.' Her mouth turned down at the corners. 'But think of the alternative, Beth. You know what that is. Dependency.' She almost spat the last word. She leapt up the back steps two at a time, turning before going inside. 'No, marry him and be done with it, that's my advice.'

Chapter 20

No, I will not let it rest

Dinner at Carter Lodge was usually something special; however, the atmosphere was subdued on this occasion.

'Mr Justice Wood, so pleased to see you again,' Mrs Burbridge responded to his distracted greeting. 'Griffith.' She nodded as Griffith gave her a perfunctory kiss on the cheek. 'But where is Mary? Where is our new Mrs Burbridge? After all, this dinner is in her honour.'

'She's mortified that she can't come down, Mama. She's entirely too unwell, and the doctor has forbidden it. She sends you all her love.'

Mrs Burbridge gave Griffith a long look before moving on to greet the other guests. 'Baron von Hügel,' she said. 'It has been too long. I know we are all …' She glanced in the direction of Rose. 'Longing to hear about the discoveries you made on your trip to New Zealand.'

The McPhails had also been invited so, despite Mr Justice Wood and Griffith being rather quieter than usual, the conversation moved along.

'Are you a racing man?' Mrs McPhail posed to the baron. 'Mr McPhail plans to meet Mr Burbridge at the race meeting. I go to the picnic meetings, of course, as do most ladies, but Mr McPhail says the serious racing is to be had at the main events.'

'I am not much of a gambler,' said von Hügel.

'That is a shame,' said Henrietta. 'I thought there might be cards after dinner.'

'Careful,' said Griffith, 'she's a veritable card sharp. I would be a rich man if I had never played cards with my sister.'

'Ah, cards,' said von Hügel. 'You have a measure of control over your fate with cards. With horses, that is a different story. I only bet on a horse if I am the rider.'

'Oh, I never even know which one I'm betting on,' Mrs McPhail chatted on. 'I leave all that to Mr McPhail.'

'And how do you fare?' Henrietta's eyebrow lifted a fraction.

The dining room was elegant but so small that there was little room left for the servants to place and replace plates as the dinner progressed. The guests' elbows rubbed against each other to general irritation.

However, Rose looked thrilled to sit beside von Hügel again, and she took every opportunity to engage his attention on botanical matters. 'But did you find the seed pods you were after? They are so tiny that—'

'Yes, yes. And not so hard if you know to look under the leaf.'

'Oh, I had thought to find them ...'

However, the baron's countenance lacked the level of interest he'd shown before.

Beth wondered if, as the time grew nearer to him leaving, whether this was due to sadness or detachment.

At the other end of the table, Mr Piggott was drinking heavily, barely touching his food. He and Mr Burbridge had been arguing in quiet voices throughout the dinner.

'I tell you sir, enough is enough. There is a moral right here.'

'And I tell you, Piggott, clearly your father and mother recognised that they were clearing the debt they owed to us in providing support for the building of Aylesford villa.'

Mrs Burbridge gave her husband a look that suggested that this was not the time to be talking about such things.

He was either not paying attention or didn't care. Mr Burbridge appealed to their host. 'You're a legal man, what do you say?'

Mr Justice Wood shrugged. 'I'm sure I can't be giving an opinion when I am so unaware of the matter.

Perhaps you should be setting about employing Mr Manning to give you an opinion.'

'Lawyers,' scoffed Mr Burbridge. The red in his cheeks had spread to his nose. 'I don't have the money to throw around to get the right of it, when I know what it is. Why, in every dispute I've ever had, the only ones to come out on the correct side of the balance sheet have been those vultures. That business with Macarthur alone cost ...'

The talk around the table resumed more generally. Mr Piggott subsided into his glass as the low monotone from that end of the table indicated that Mr Burbridge was continuing his thesis without interruption.

At her end, Mrs McPhail was valiantly trying to keep the conversation going. 'What are your thoughts on the marriage in the court of Hungary, Mrs Burbridge?' She looked towards Baron von Hügel. 'I was reading all about Prince Metternich in the papers. But perhaps the baron, being from there, would know more about it?'

Rose's sharply indrawn breath was audible. Everyone at the table, it seemed, apart from Mrs McPhail, knew the baron's history of love lost. Mrs McPhail looked blankly from face to face.

The baron spoke quietly, but composedly. 'That is the difficulty with living so far away from the world, I think. Your newspapers are filled with events that occurred so long ago. By the time you hear of it, the events themselves are history.'

'Oh, but we are quite up to date—' began Mrs McPhail defensively.

'It is not right, sir,' shouted Mr Piggott jumping to his feet.

Henrietta and Griffith exchanged looks of alarm.

'How about we let the matter rest, Cousin Arthur,' Griffith said soothingly, his hand resting on Piggott's shoulder.

Piggott shook him off. 'No, I will not let it rest. I have let it rest for long enough. We cannot move forward in this matter.' He gave an unconscious glance in Beth's direction. 'Until, at the very least, my uncle acknowledges his debt to my father's estate. Mr Wood, I implore you.'

'Sit down, there's a good chap,' said Mr Justice Wood. 'I always find a cigar and brandy bring things into perspective.'

Baron von Hügel rose to his feet. 'I must give my apologies. I still have some work to do on my paper for my presentation to the Society later this evening. My thanks for all your hospitality.' As he left, he gave a formal little bow to Rose.

Mrs Burbridge rose to her feet, and at her signal, the ladies retired to the drawing room. They sat there making a few half-hearted attempts at conversation. Eventually, Henrietta gave up altogether and went to the piano and picked out a few airs.

'It's worrying that Mary couldn't be with us,' said Mrs McPhail, the only person untroubled by the argument in the other room. 'Though, perhaps it'll be a blessing? My aunt's cousin was ill for the entire time, right up until ...'

Mrs Burbridge could usually be relied upon to join in a discussion of anticipated blessings from marriage, but even she couldn't be engaged on the topic.

'Griffith seemed worried about her,' volunteered Beth, stepping in. 'Rose, didn't you think so?'

'Mm?' Rose had been staring into the middle distance.

'Well, it's hard for a gentleman to have to dine without his wife,' said Mrs McPhail. 'I always think it's a great pity to see married men in society without their wives. I always say the same thing to Mr McPhail about Captain Piper. Captain Piper, I say, should set about marrying a proper sort of woman so that she can be beside him when he entertains. Now, I know—I hope I don't offend you—I know that common-law wives were more often the rule in the colony in the early days, but really these days we are perfectly civilised. Even if we are on the other side of the world and not entirely up to date.'

The door of the drawing room opened and Griffith entered with his father-in-law. 'Mama, Father has ordered the carriage and means for you all to stay at Pulteney's Hotel rather than with us. Mr Piggott will be staying here.'

'My apologies, Mrs Burbridge,' said Mr Justice Wood, 'but family matters, as always, have proved to be the most vexatious. Perhaps another time.' He looked genuinely saddened.

Chapter 21

I'm a complete fool

Mr Burbridge was attacking his breakfast sausages with murderous intent. 'How dare the man, how dare he?' he expostulated.

Beth watched with growing queasiness the fat oozing across her father's plate. She assumed he was talking about Mr Piggott. She pushed her toast aside.

Mrs Burbridge was silent, steadily chewing. She looked like she had heard the argument one too many times.

'The arrogance of an Irishman like Giles Wood, thinking he can tell me my business,' Mr Burbidge went on. 'If Griffith hadn't married into the family, why I'd—' He broke off, savagely biting off the end of the sausage.

He was referring to Mr Justice Wood, Beth realised to her disappointment. 'What did he say?" she asked, stepping in for her mother.

'His lord high and mighty says that what we may or may not have been owed to us from your grandmother's estate is a completely separate matter to the money that your Uncle Piggott lent us towards

Aylesford. I ask you, how can that be? It's as plain as day: money owed is money owed.'

'Perhaps, if Mr Piggott—' Mrs Burbridge spoke in a quiet, soothing tone.

'Not another word about that man,' shouted Mr Burbridge, too loudly even for him, as he winced and continued more quietly, though no less fiercely. 'There will be no more scheming,' he said, looking directly at his wife. 'We will be fighting him in the courts, and there's an end to it.'

Did that mean …? Beth felt a rush of relief. Immediately, she regretted her selfishness. Her father's complexion shone with a waxy sheen. His eyes were bloodshot and he was breathing heavily. She looked worriedly to her mother.

Mrs Burbridge gave an almost imperceptible shake of her head. Do nothing, he'll calm down if left to work it out, it said.

Beth looked from her father's departing back to her mother. 'Has Rose been down yet?' Beth asked.

'He's off to the races,' her mother said.

'Yes, but …?'

'Rose and Henrietta took it upon themselves to go back to Carter Lodge last night,' she said between gritted teeth. 'Worried about Mary, apparently. They've sent a note.' She indicated the folded paper beside her plate. 'They'll collect us both for Aylesford shortly. You'd better hurry your breakfast along.'

Aylesford was very quiet. Most of the men had been granted leave to attend the race day, so the yards were still. In the heat of the day, the cattle were grazing at the far edges of their paddocks where the best shade could be found. The only sounds were the everyday noises as the servants went about their duties.

Out in the kitchen, Mrs Holder was making bread. Her huffs and puffs as she kneaded were interspersed with the loud flopping of the dough as she beat it into submission. Susan and Martha were upstairs seeing to the rooms. Their footsteps mapped their tasks: Susan's light tip-tap as she moved about the rooms tidying up after her mistresses, and Martha's heavy footfall as she cleaned and polished. They were both being quieter than usual, as Mrs Burbridge had one of her migraines and was resting in her room, blinds drawn.

Beth sat in the drawing room trying to apply herself to her drawing. The light was not good in this room at this time of day. Generally she would have relocated to one of the lounges on the verandah, but the events of the night before had unsettled her. She needed to talk about them with someone. So far, neither Rose nor Henrietta had said a word.

Rose was affecting to read but hadn't turned a page for some time. Henrietta was playing a piece on the piano but kept making a mistake at the same place and then going over the section again and again.

'Must you, Henrietta?' Rose said sharply.

'There's only one way to get it right,' said Henrietta, affecting the heavy German accent of their former music master. She did the same section again.

Rose sighed heavily and resumed staring at the page in front of her.

'Oh, I can't stand it.' Henrietta slammed the lid of the piano down. The keys jangled in protest. 'I'm going for a walk.' Her footsteps disappeared down the hall and then resounded faintly across the back verandah, disappearing as she strode away from the house.

Rose looked up from her page. There were tears in her eyes.

'What's wrong?' Beth found herself whispering, even though there was no one to hear.

Rose blinked furiously. 'I'm a complete fool.'

'Sorry?'

Rose took a deep breath. 'I went to the Society's meeting last night.'

'What? No. Why?'

'I thought Charles, Baron von Hügel I mean, had invited me. Don't look at me like that. You were there. He kept mentioning it, and every time he'd look at me in that way he has, so intently. I was sure he meant that I could go along, that I'd be welcome.'

Beth tried to think back. She had heard the baron mention the Society meeting several times, but her recall of the conversation was vague. 'So you went?'

'I walked down to the Gardens from Pulteney's. It was still fairly early in the evening and, since we'd come back so soon from Carter Lodge, there were people about. I went first to the Society's rooms. They were open, with everything set up in readiness, but no one had arrived. I didn't want to have to explain myself until the baron could introduce me, so I went into a little vestibule off the entrance and waited. As they all started to arrive, I realised that none of them had brought their wives. I knew that it would be mainly men, of course, but I didn't realise … and if I had, well I would never have gone.'

'Of course not.'

'Finally, he came. But I couldn't go out, could I? I would have embarrassed him in front of everyone.' She wiped her eyes. 'And myself, of course.'

'So, no one saw you?' said Beth. 'No harm was done?'

'No, not then.'

Beth waited, fearful of what she might hear.

'I stayed there all through the meeting. After they'd all left, I was worried the gates would shut. I slipped out, thinking to walk back to the hotel, but it was dark and the people on the streets were the very worst sort of men. I was walking as quickly as I could when a man called out from a group of them, hanging around a cook fire. "Is it a ride you'll be wanting then, missy? Always happy to oblige," he said. And he did this awful gesture.'

Beth's stomach turned.

'I didn't know what to do. A few of them began to walk over. Then … then a carriage stopped, and …' She shook her head. 'It was Henrietta. She'd been worrying about Griffith, you see, and couldn't sleep. Eventually, she'd gone down and got the night porter to order a carriage and was headed to Carter Lodge.'

'So it all turned out all right, really.'

'Yes, I suppose so.' Rose put aside the book that had stayed so long ignored on her lap. 'I need to get outside. Let's get White to saddle the horses.'

They rode together along the bridle track that circled past the Ridgeways' cottage. At the point where the track began to head back to the house, they paused and dismounted, leading the horses slowly, eking out each minute they could spend away from the house.

Abruptly, as though they had been speaking, Rose turned to Beth. 'But, Beth, as I waited and waited and then realised that I might have to stay out all night, and it was all for nothing, I found I didn't care what people thought. I had done everything I could for the man I loved and I would have done much more.' She said the last words defiantly, almost daring Beth to condemn her.

But ever since Beth had seen Henrietta with de Bougainville, nothing could ever strike her with the same force again. This was the truth about the world of men and women—a truth that she'd never wanted to know, a truth that she saw now that she had done all that she could to avoid knowing. As she watched Rose's misery, she realised that she felt no sympathy. It was not that she judged her. She had condemned Henrietta with a righteous anger and fury, but here was Rose—desperate and declaring that she would have spent the night alone with von Hügel.

'Oh, Rose,' she said, shaking her head at her sister's foolishness.

They were quiet for a moment.

'Henrietta thinks it amusing, you know,' Rose continued. 'I'm sure she'd turn it into one of her oh-so-charming anecdotes, except for … well, let's just say.' Her gaze hardened as she looked Beth in the face. 'Secrets can be a mutual obligation.'

Beth stared back, trying to read her mind.

'Henrietta has her own secret about the Gardens, as it turns out,' Rose said.

Beth waited for her to continue.

'That was where she'd planned to meet de Bougainville last time she was here. Though perhaps you knew that? She and de Bougainville were to meet there, at midnight, so he could ferry her out to *L'Ésperance.* I don't think de Bougainville has any idea of how unsafe the streets are here to even suggest such a thing.'

'Romantic, though,' said Beth, remembering her mother's words about Frenchmen.

'Well, yes, I suppose. But who do you think turned up?'

Rose was clearly enjoying turning Henrietta's affair into an anecdote herself. Perhaps it took the sting out of her own tale.

Beth shook her head numbly. 'Papa.'

'No, Mr Richeley, pacing up and down the jetty. But he didn't see her.'

'And de Bougainville didn't come?'

'No. Henrietta's sure he would have, but he must have seen Richeley and thought the better of it.'

Beth thought she should have been relieved. Papa had told Mr Richeley to deal with it. There had never been any prospect that her father might have had a duel. She'd been as naïve as Rose, yet their foolishness made them both as dangerous as Henrietta.

The house in view, they remounted, each lost in thoughts.

'It must have been late by the time you got to Carter Lodge,' Beth said, turning over the events in her mind.

'Yes.' Rose shut her eyes at the memory. 'Anyway, we thought to see if we could wake Griffith and he'd let us in, but the household was still up, because Mary had taken a turn for the worse. And it was Mr Wood himself who we had to speak to.'

'Didn't he think it was odd, you both turning up like that?'

'Yes, but you know Henrietta. So charming. But the way Mr Justice Wood looked at me.' She gave a small shiver. 'I felt like I was a lying witness, or worse.' Rose shrugged as if to shed her embarrassment. She flicked the reins and put Blackie into a trot.

Chapter 22

Stop or I'll shoot

As they rode into the yard, Beth mulled over what Rose had told her. Her thoughts were broken by shouts coming from the house. They left the horses, reins looped over the rail, and ran towards the noise.

Susan called from the steps, 'It's Mr Burbridge, he needs help. Bushrangers, it's bushrangers.' She was white-faced with terror.

Beth saw Jack, doubled up, his hands on his knees, trying to catch his breath.

Rose took charge. 'What's happened, Jack? Quickly.'

'Down by the main gate, Miss. Four of 'em, armed—they dragged Mr Chapman down from the box and tied 'im up. And then they got Mr Burbridge out with their guns pointed straight at 'im. But I was havin' a kip on the back, see, so they didn't see me and I got away. O'Reilly and Matthews have to go and help.'

'They're not back from the races yet.' Rose looked at Beth. 'There's only us. We've got to go.'

'But we can't … I can't … You and Henrietta …'

'Goodness knows where Henrietta's got to. Jack, go and see if you can find her. Tell her what's happened—

she was headed down to the river earlier.' Rose whirled on Beth. 'Come on.' She ran back to the yard.

Beth hesitated. *What does Rose think I can do?* Armed robbers against two unarmed women and one man. A man well past his prime, she thought with a stab of realisation. The man who preferred to ride in a carriage even when, like today, he was the sole occupant. Then she was running too.

Rose hoisted herself onto the lower rung of the rail and mounted.

Within seconds, Beth was mounted too and walking her horse out onto the open ground. She and Rose simultaneously urged their horses into a canter. Then Rose put Blackie into a gallop and, as Star followed, Beth gripped with her thighs, praying that she wouldn't fall.

The carriage came into sight, and Beth saw that the men were on foot, no horses in sight. Mr Burbridge had been forced into a kneeling position, his hands behind his head, beside the trussed body of the coachman lying on the ground. A rough-looking man with a heavy beard was gesticulating angrily at Mr Burbridge with one hand and waving his gun in his face with the other. Two others had hauled their father's valise down out from the carriage and were crouched beside it, scrabbling through its contents. Jack had said there were four of them. Where was the fourth man?

Then Rose was yelling and whooping at the top of her lungs and urging her horse to go faster still. Beth had no idea what Rose was shouting and doubted whether Rose herself knew, but her own horse had redoubled its efforts without Beth doing a thing.

The three men looked around, mouths agape, but the hand of the man holding the pistol at their father's head didn't waver.

One of the men who'd been looting their father's bag grabbed his musket, which he'd lain beside him, and stood and took aim. 'Stop or I'll shoot,' he shouted.

Rose didn't check her pace; she rode on regardless. Her hair had flown loose and streamed out behind her wildly, and she charged at the three men—one hand with reins wrapped tightly, the other grasping her horse's mane.

And then Beth saw the fourth man coming out from behind the carriage, adjusting his trousers. His musket was leaning against the side of the carriage where he'd left it.

Then Beth found she was shouting too. She tugged at Star's reins so that she was riding directly at the fourth man, her voice so high and loud it resounded inside her head like a clarion.

The bearded man shouted, 'They'll have others behind 'em. Get out before they get 'ere.' Without waiting for the rest of the gang, he raced back into the bushes.

Seeing their leader fleeing, the other three ran after him.

Rose swung off her horse. 'Papa, are you harmed?'

Beth slowed Star to a walk. She slid off and moved over to her father. His face was white.

'Whatever did you think you were doing?' His jaw was clenched, and he kept shaking his head as if some thought needed to be dislodged.

They untied Mr Chapman and settled him inside the carriage, as he was too shaken to ride or walk, let alone drive the carriage. Rose, by dint of roping her own horse alongside the lead horse, managed to get the carriage moving again and up to the house. Beth walked slowly alongside her father because he refused to get into the carriage. It seemed to take forever, compared with how little time had passed between leaping on their horses to get there.

Had she really ridden so fast? She found it barely credible. And they'd chased off the bushrangers. She had thought she knew all about fear, but she'd never experienced its like before. It coursed through her veins like lightning bolts that powered something she realised must be courage.

She glanced at her father beside her. She'd expected rage, of course, but she had thought it might quickly turn to gratitude once he'd got past the initial shock. But he had said nothing else beyond his first shout. He was trembling with the effort of walking as they approached the house.

Mrs Burbridge was standing, wringing her hands, at the front steps.

There was a flurry of activity as the house servants ran to help get Mr Burbridge inside and help the coachman around to the kitchen, where Mrs Holder was promising him a 'good stiff drink'.

As Jack set about unhitching the carriage and sorting out the care of the horses, Beth stood beside Star, patting her, murmuring her thanks. She turned to find Henrietta behind her, her eyes taking in the sight of Beth's horse, streaming with sweat. She gave Beth a quick nod of approbation and linked her arm through Beth's to walk back into the house.

As the two of them walked together, a calm descended upon Beth such as she had never known. They paused before entering, watching their father being ushered upstairs under the watchful eye of Mrs Burbridge. He needed both Martha and Susan to help him; he was shaking so much.

'So, talking with Rose last night, I am left with a small mystery, dearest Beth,' said Henrietta silkily in her ear, 'and that is, how Papa and Mr Richeley came to find out about my private plans all those years ago.'

For a few days after the robbery, Mr Burbridge barely stirred from his room. Mrs Burbridge attended him personally, and Susan and Martha remained close-lipped as to his condition, clearly under threats of dismissal from Mrs Burbridge if they were to do otherwise.

Beth, having seen how shaken he'd been immediately after it all, was not concerned when he remained upstairs on the following day. But as the days became weeks, she became increasingly concerned as to why he would continue to suffer so. When she pursued the matter with her mother, Mrs Burbridge made vague allusions to a recurrence of 'his old trouble' and Beth thought perhaps it might be the gout. Certainly, he was as easily vexed as he always was when he did have the gout. Susan and Martha often left his room in tears after having been shouted at for such offences as clearing the chamber-pot too loudly. So, was it only the gout that was troubling him so much?

It was a relief when their brother Bill finally arrived from the Hunter properties. For his eldest son, Mr Burbridge managed to come downstairs.

But Bill had arrived with an unexpected companion: Baron von Hügel.

Rose froze when she first saw him, and Beth felt her embarrassment. Somehow it didn't matter that the baron was unaware of the events that surrounded his Society meeting. The discomfort was intense.

'Had to drag this poor blighter out of the creek,' Bill guffawed, clapping von Hügel soundly on the back.

The baron flinched under the assault.

Beth couldn't imagine a more dissimilar pairing than her brother, who adopted the rough dress and speech of the currency lads when working the property, and the baron, in his elegant European sophistication.

'Yes, I was indeed most fortunate,' said von Hügel. 'I had left the rest of my party back at the turn, thinking to see the falls there. But the waters were deeper than I had been led to believe, and so—'

'We've had a fine old time,' Bill interrupted. 'Managed to effect some introductions with a few of the local blacks—'

'They were most helpful.' It was von Hügel's turn to interrupt. He seemed anxious to head Bill off from his story. 'Their knowledge of the native flora—'

'Well, I tell you, it was the funniest thing I've seen in a long time.' Bill leaned forward in his chair. 'See, while the baron was drying off a bit, I realised that some of the mob were skulking around in the bush nearby, so I excused myself and had a quiet word with Jacko, who's by way of being a good mate of mine so long as I keep up his supply of tobacco and sugar.'

Mr Burbridge nodded his head as if endorsing Bill's comment from his own experience.

As Bill continued his tale, Beth could see that Rose, her eyes fixed on the baron, dreaded the end, but the telling was too compelling to interrupt.

'Well, the blacks have this habit of smearing every inch of their bodies with goanna fat when the mosquitoes are getting bad, so I says to Jacko, "that water's really brought out the bloody dibing", if you'll excuse the language,' he added for the benefit of his sisters. 'I says, "I don't think my friend the baron likes them much." And Jacko, well, he catches my drift, and he says, "I never met me a baron before, boss—think I should give him a real bush welcome".'

At this stage in the story, Mr Burbridge was laughing so hard at his son's tale that his face was purpling.

'So, that's what he did, didn't he? Came right up and wrapped his greasy body around our friend the baron here, in a real bear hug.' Bill grinned at the memory. 'My eyes were watering at the stink all the way back. But,' he added, 'we didn't have any mosquito problems after that, did we?'

Rose, her own embarrassment forgotten, reached out a hand in sympathy to the baron and then quickly withdrew it.

The baron, his expression rigidly polite, clearly had had enough of being the butt of Bill's humour. 'I hear there has been much excitement here, Miss Burbridge, during my absence,' he said. 'I hear you are quite the heroine. And your sister, Miss Beth, too, of course.'

'Nothing of the sort,' roared Mr Burbridge, his elevated mood gone, engulfed in a wave of fury. He was on his feet and his mouth was moving as though struggling to speak.

Mrs Burbridge was beside him in an instant.

Her husband shook her off. 'Recklessness, that's what it was, complete recklessness,' he shouted before abruptly walking out.

'It's all been a bit tiring, what with the company,' Mrs Burbridge said weakly before following.

Chapter 23

We have company

Beth was waiting by the bedroom window for Rose to get ready when Henrietta wandered past, still in her wrapper.

'Oh, are you two riding? Wait on and I'll join you. Where's Susan got to? I need some help with my boots.'

Rose mouthed, 'She'll take forever.'

Beth, fighting back a smirk, relished the feeling of camaraderie between them.

'We'll see you down there,' Rose replied and moved on to lacing her own boots.

Beth turned again to the window. 'Oh, no. We have company.'

They both looked out the window at the barouche in the distance. The hood was down, revealing two men—one top hat, one old-fashioned three-cornered hat.

'Who? Oh. Mr Wood.' Rose was blushing. 'Why has he come?'

The other man was Cousin Arthur. Beth feared she knew why he had come and why he'd brought Mr Justice Wood along. Perhaps her cousin was under the illusion that Mr Burbridge would have calmed down sufficiently to hear reason. Mr Justice Wood, being a reasonable man, might well think likewise.

Henrietta, one foot draped in an unlaced boot, hopped to the window beside them. 'Giles Wood is proving to be an extraordinarily supportive father-in-law to Griffith, that's all I can say.'

'You think they'll be here about the debt?' Rose looked relieved.

Henrietta looked from one to the other. 'Possibly. Probably. And likely even for matters matrimonial as well. Now, my dears.' She adopted a mock-maternal tone. 'If I may paraphrase something I once heard dear Uncle Piggott say: there comes a time when every woman needs to settle down—later for some, of course, but still—'

'I don't want to see him,' Beth said.

'But it's too soon after his wife's passing, surely?' Rose said at the same time. 'You go down, Beth. Tell Mama I've already left to go riding. Please,' she said, seeing Beth's face reflecting her own panic. 'I'll go out the back once they're in the drawing room.'

Beth tried to calm her nerves. As long as Mama was in the room, then everything would be all right. Nothing of a personal nature would arise. As she began to descend the stairs, she saw her father emerge from the library below. She hesitated mid-step. Mr Burbridge didn't see her.

Her father walked along the side of the hall, one finger running along the cedar panelling. It glowed red-gold in the shafts of morning sun coming through the decorative fanlight above the doorway. The sounds of gravel crunching under the carriage wheels made him turn and stride back. He paused by the burnished balustrade, one hand smoothed the surface. Looking up, he saw her. His face was impassive. And then he retreated, the library doors closed behind him.

Beth reached the drawing room before the guests had been ushered through the front door. She slid into a chair beside her mother, picking up her embroidery. Her hands were shaking too much to do more than hold the needle above the cloth. Mrs Burbridge was similarly inattentive.

Susan entered and did her usual bob—part curtsey, part insolence. 'Mr Justice Wood and Mr Piggott, ma'am, to see Mr Burbridge.'

Mrs Burbridge's lips tightened. She shook her head in worried indecision and then said, 'Show the gentlemen in here. I'll go and let Mr Burbridge know.'

Beth did her best to remain calm as the two men greeted her. Neither looked as though they expected to stay in the drawing room for long. Neither spoke.

'And how might Mary be faring, Mr Wood? We have all been worried about her.'

The grey shadow that passed over Wood's face told her how dismally she'd failed to find a safe topic.

'Not well, I'm afraid,' Mr Wood replied then said no more.

Before Beth could think of another question, her mother returned.

'Mr Burbridge can see you in the library, Mr Wood. Susan will show you through.'

Mr Wood got to his feet with a farewell nod to Beth.

As Mr Piggott began to rise, Mrs Burbridge spoke again. 'I am most sorry, Mr Piggott. But Mr Burbridge would prefer to see Mr Justice Wood alone.'

'He will not see me?' Mr Piggott sat down, this time sinking against the back of the chair.

'No.' Her mother looked genuinely concerned but made no attempt at all to smooth Mr Piggott's discomfort.

The voices coming from the library were a low murmur.

'Where might Rose be, Beth?' Mrs Burbridge broke the silence at last. 'Would you be so kind as to suggest she join us?'

Grateful for the chance to leave, Beth abandoned her needlework.

She paused as she passed the library door.

'What secrets are you divining now, Beth?' Henrietta was right behind her.

'Nothing,' Beth whispered. 'Mr Wood is talking with Papa in there.'

Henrietta drew Beth back behind the stairs and lowered her voice. 'Is it about the money Papa keeps refusing to pay?'

Beth shook her head. 'It's about Rose, I think.'

'Never,' Mr Burbridge's voice resounded down the hall as he flung open the door. 'Never, do you hear?'

Beth and Henrietta both stepped out into the hall to see Mrs Burbridge almost running towards them.

'Beth, get back to Mr Piggott, this instant, in the drawing room,' she said, pulling up short, struggling to regain her breath.

Mr Wood was walking out of the library. Mr Burbridge had retired back inside.

Mrs Burbridge continued, her voice high and bright, 'And Henrietta, I'm sure Mr Wood would be interested to see the, the—' but here she clearly ran out of ideas.

'Yes, of course, Mama,' said Henrietta. 'I'm sure he would be most interested. Mr Wood, I'm sure you have a fine appreciation of such matters ...' Henrietta's voice trailed into the distance as she ushered Mr Wood, either too polite or too angry to resist, out to the back garden.

Beth waited until she heard the library door close behind her mother, and then taking a deep breath, she went back into the drawing room.

Her needle had lost its thread, and she ran the silken fibre through her fingers to the tip and edged it through the eye. She held the needle between her finger and thumb, poised above the heart of the rose she was working on.

Mr Piggott sat mutely.

Beth didn't want to look directly at him. He was watching her.

'I must apologise for my silence, Cousin Arthur, but you have come upon us in a moment of some confusion.'

'I fear I may be partly to blame.'

She looked up, grateful that he at least was not angry, unlike her father and Mr Wood.

'As you know, Mr Justice Wood has lent a sympathetic ear to my situation. So, he undertook to make some representations on my behalf to your father. I think the shouting was your father's response, unfortunately.'

Beth inserted her needle, careful to count the number of spaces along the weave before bringing the needle back up through the cloth and slowly drawing through the thread. So, she thought, Mr Piggott too had thought the conversation in the library was all about him. But perhaps Mr Wood had been pursuing his own interests. She was almost sorry for her cousin. She patted the sewn thread into smooth alignment with its fellows.

'But I had a most interesting conversation with your mother.' He then went on. 'She is a remarkable woman. I confess I could never understand how such an amazing creature as Cousin Henrietta came to be, but now all is explained.'

Beth moved her needle into position for the next stitch.

'I hope you don't mind if I speak as frankly to you as your mother has done with me. She suggested that if you and I were to —'

Beth's needle thrust into the cloth and pierced her finger. She felt its pain but left it there.

He leaned forward, reformulating his address. 'If you were to consider the prospect of becoming my wife, then I could … Well, I would, of course, be the happiest of men. And, as a member of the family, new partnerships could be developed to strengthen the financial future of both our families, ahem, in these uncertain times.' He had finished. He sat back in his chair again.

Beth pulled the needle back out and watched as the spot of blood seeped through the rose to stain the cloth deep crimson. 'My father is adamant —' she began.

'That's what I said too.' Mr Piggott smiled, apparently pleased that they were of one mind so soon.

'But, your mother thinks that he will come around to the idea. I have noticed, if you'll forgive the observation, that your father usually does as your mother advises.'

Beth nodded numbly. Her cousin's observations were entirely accurate. From her own interview with her parents, she knew that her mother had already won this battle. If Mrs Burbridge pretended it were up to her husband, then it was for show, to acknowledge him as the head of the family. 'Thank you,' she said finally, setting down her embroidery. 'Thank you for being so frank.. You have given me much to think about, Cousin Arthur. I do need some time, and to talk with my parents, I'm sure you understand.'

'Yes, indeed.' Mr Piggott looked the happiest she'd seen him since his arrival. 'Take all the time you need. Though, not too long. Matters to attend to back in the real world, you know.'

Beth knew that by 'the real world' he meant the northern hemisphere. It struck her for the first time that this marriage would mean leaving the place she had been born.

He laughed nervously. 'Passages to book, of course. Couldn't have us in the berths they give the single fellows, could I?'

And there it was—the other reality that marriage would mean.

'If you will excuse me—' She rose to her feet awkwardly, her sewing falling from her lap.

'Of course, of course,' stammered Mr Piggott. 'I shall await Mr Wood by the carriage.'

She looked down at the crumpled fabric on the floor, the thread loose, the needle gone.

She let it lie.

Beth had barely gone two steps when she saw Henrietta coming down the hall with Rose and Mr Wood. She couldn't face being seen. She drew into the shadows under the stairs.

Henrietta, almost as tall as Mr Wood, was laughing at something he was saying. *Henrietta really can't help but flirt,* Beth thought.

'Oh yes,' Henrietta said. 'Loves to ride, our Rose, when she's not collecting wildflowers that is.'

Rose's face was stony.

As they drew level with the drawing room, Henrietta said, 'Jack should be back with the mail. I hope you'll excuse me if I don't stay and play chaperone, I'm rather expecting a letter.' Her eyes danced between them.

Mr Justice Wood looked uncharacteristically ill at ease. He stood by the drawing room door, one hand extended as if to invite Rose to accompany him. They entered, the door remaining an inch ajar, for propriety's sake.

Beth went to step out from the darkness, hoping to slip up the stairs unnoticed. Henrietta was still standing in the hallway. She stood before the mirror, slowly repositioning her hairpins. Beth realised that Henrietta had no intention of moving away until she'd heard what Mr Wood had to discuss with Rose. Beth sank back against the wall, wishing she didn't have to hear, but compelled to listen all the same.

'Horses are such demanding beasts, aren't they?' Mr Wood was saying.

'It's a question of knowing what they want,' Rose replied.

'Do you know what you want, Miss Burbridge?'

There was a long pause.

'I have been speaking with your father,' he began. 'No, not about the other night. We humans are emotional beings, are we not? Our emotions can prove to be mighty unreliable guides, however. What really matters are the rational decisions we make. Though, to tell the truth, I'm not entirely sure what your father is using as a guide right now. However, I thought I'd do the right thing and talk to him first—although neither of us are of an age where such a step is necessary.'

'Do you like riding, Mr Wood?'

Mr Wood didn't appear taken aback by her inconsequential remark. 'Not in the least. Walking takes a lot longer of course, but you do meet some interesting folk along the way, so it's all time well spent.' He paused for a moment. 'So back to what I was saying. I took the step of declaring my intentions of seeking your hand in marriage, my dear.' It was clear that he hadn't finished all he had to say, but he waited for Rose's reaction.

There was a light pattering from the end of the hall. Henrietta had dropped her hairpins. Beth could see her, comically frozen in mid-stoop as she bent to collect them up.

It didn't appear that the noise had penetrated into the drawing room, for Rose began to reply. 'I don't think Papa would consider—'

'No, indeed he did not. In fact, he will cut you off entirely, if you were to marry me, Rose. So that is why I asked you if you knew your own mind.'

Henrietta was picking up each hairpin, one at a time, clearly ensuring each was held firmly between thumb and forefinger and transferred to her cupped hand before she reached for the next.

Beth wanted to scream down the hall to Rose— *marry him*. Her certainty was as much a revelation to her as was the urge to shout. Mr Wood spoke of rational decisions. But rationally, Baron von Hügel—a man of distinction, a man with whom Rose shared every intellectual interest, a man who appreciated her for her intellect as much as her beauty—was a better match. But the baron had not proposed. Or perhaps this desperate feeling was simply that Beth wanted it all to be over.

Rose's voice was so quiet as to be barely audible. 'It is so soon since Mrs Wood's passing—'

'Yes, and for that reason, I seek but an indication from you. You are an attractive and intelligent woman. It is a wonder to me that you have remained unmarried for so long. If you will excuse a riding analogy from a committed pedestrian, I would not wish to be beaten to the post.'

There was a cry from outside the house. Henrietta swiftly opened the door. Jack came up the steps at a single bound, his bare feet sending the dust flying. He had a note in his hand, waving it about as he ran.

'For m'lud,' he blurted, and he could say no more, so great was his fear of all things judicial.

'I'll take it.' Henrietta's face looked concerned as she looked at the handwriting. She was down the hall and into the drawing room in seconds.

Unnoticed, Beth followed and stood by the open doorway.

'Mr Wood, it's a letter for you from Griffith.'

Mr Wood tore it open and read. 'It's Mary. My darling daughter has succumbed to her illness.'

Chapter 24

Well, you'll have to marry someone

The regatta was well underway. Every boat with a sail was out on the harbour, the brisk breeze strong enough to propel even the most reluctant vessel into the races with half a chance. The best vantage points were Dawes Point for the starts and Watsons Bay for the finishes.

Celebrating crews swung in to moor at the jetty and joined their family and friends who'd made the journey along South Head Road laden with picnic baskets in readiness to receive them. Out on the water, buoys were laid out marking the routes, and race officials were packed into boats at strategic locations to invigilate. While the betting had been getting increasingly courageous as the races had proceeded, several disputed turns had erupted into slanging matches between rival yachts already.

Even boats that were not involved directly in the races were out, parading up and down the harbour, sails billowing. In among them were the rowboats, skiffs and dinghies of everyone who could afford, share or borrow one, legally or otherwise, for the occasion.

Beth scrambled along the rocky edges to the vantage point the Burbridges had laid claim to by dint of spreading cushions and blankets. 'Where's Papa?' she asked Rose, shading her eyes against the sun.

Rose was staring fixedly at a small rock pool close by, her head bowed in concentration on the spray of barnacles—a desiccated honeycomb, dried out as the tide had receded. 'Still in the carriage,' she muttered, giving a warning glance in the direction of their mother.

Mrs Burbridge was slumped, her normally straight back bowed by the strain of the last weeks.

'Why?' mouthed Beth.

Rose shrugged.

Neither of their parents had spoken much in the carriage during the long ride from Aylesford. At intervals, Mrs Burbridge had offered her husband a blanket, which he had kept throwing off. It would do him good to get out, she had said.

Mr Burbridge had continued keeping to his room except when pressured by his wife. Beth had been grateful for his seclusion at first. While he was absent, the subject of Mr Piggott's proposal would remain in abeyance. Her mother had plagued her with questions, of course, but Beth had fended her off, saying she wanted to seek her father's advice, and since he was not seeing anyone apart from his wife, and even seeing her on sufferance, Beth found herself on an island of respite.

She knew the tide would rise again and wash her from her place of safety very soon. She'd seen Mr Piggott's name listed on the passenger list in the paper for the *Marquis of Huntley*, which was scheduled for departure before the month was out. Sometimes, she deluded herself that he would sail away without another word about her or about the debt. Perhaps that's what her father thought too. But if she knew anything about her cousin after their brief acquaintance, it was that he was as dogged as her father was stubborn. He would want his answer.

What she had not counted on was his presence at Watsons Bay. She should have anticipated it, she realised. He had come with the Woods — the family out in society for the first time since Mary's death. Their party had settled themselves further away from the water, closer to the trees. Mr Justice Wood and Griffith were walking together slowly, deep in conversation. Henrietta's children had rushed to play with the Wood children, and their cheerful shrieks contrasted oddly with the sombre dress of the adults.

Henrietta had been chatting to different groups of picnickers, and Beth saw her pause for a word with Mr Piggott. In response to something he said, she pointed in Beth's direction.

'I might go and see how Papa is getting along,' Beth said.

Mrs Burbridge gave no sign that she'd heard.

'Rose?'

'What?' Rose looked up. 'Oh. I'll walk with you a bit. Why we had to sit on such hard rocks, I don't know. I haven't seen Baron von Hügel, have you?'

'I saw him talking with Mr Wood earlier.'

'So amusing.'

Beth smiled. The only good thing to come out of the recent events was that Rose had reverted to her usual tetchy self after months of moody longing.

'You should marry Mr Piggott,' Rose blurted suddenly.

'What? You, of all people, should understand my situation.'

'Well, you'll have to marry someone. He could be worse. Think of Mr Babcock.'

Beth couldn't help but laugh.

They walked a little further.

'What if I don't want to be married, ever?' Beth asked.

'No, how can you think that? A marriage may be one forged from necessity, yet affection will grow and, even if not, there will be children to love. Is it a life, to have no one to love?' All traces of irascible Rose had gone. Her voice vibrated with the intensity of her emotion.

Beth scrutinised her. 'And how does this not apply to your own situation?'

Rose stared at her in amazement. 'Because I do love,' she said simply.

It took Beth a while for Rose's words to sink in. Did she mean to imply that Beth was a loveless person: someone who no one could love, or someone who loved no one, or perhaps both? *But I do love*, her mind shrieked so loudly that she thought she had shouted the words aloud. She stared at Rose as if seeing her for first time. A twitch of the lips, flick of the eyes, and there it was—pity. Rose, wrapped up in her own smug cloak of unrequited yearning, felt sorry for her. Beth stood, shaking her head numbly.

Rose gave a little shrug and headed back to the water to where Baron von Hügel had joined Mrs Burbridge.

Beth took a few steps to follow, then quickly took a few more in a different direction. She should go to Papa. He couldn't stay cooped up alone in the carriage all afternoon. He should have something to eat, at least.

'Miss Beth.'

She jumped. 'Mr Piggott.'

'You seemed lost in in your thoughts. I'm sorry to be disturbing them.' He was clearly taking care to speak slowly and considerately, like a rider holding back on the reins. His hat was jammed down past the tips of his ears, so as to prevent the gusty wind from blowing it off. It gave him a comical appearance, his eyebrows lost in the rim.

Beth searched her feelings. She knew she didn't love him, but that was hardly a prerequisite for marriage. When she'd first met him, she'd been predisposed to feel cousinly affection and found his dress and manners quaint. When the prospect of marriage had arisen, she'd been overcome with a revulsion she couldn't explain. He was no more or less than any other man. Objectively she knew he was no match for the manly figures of de Bougainville or von Hügel, but that was hardly his fault any more than it was her fault for not being as pretty as Rose or as striking as Henrietta. But, looking at him now, could she grow to love him?

Mr Piggott was continuing to talk in the deliberate manner he had adopted. 'And so, Miss Beth, I have the opportunity to take up a position with Palmer and Company. Apparently, my agency experience will be an asset in Canton. Or,' he said, searching her face, 'or, or London, if you should prefer it. However, I need to settle my father's affairs and my own before I leave.' He took a deep breath. 'So, Miss Beth—'

'Oh, Papa has decided to join us,' Beth exclaimed, seeing her father's hand emerge from the carriage window to reach around to open the door. 'You will excuse me, I'm sure.' Beth walked away rapidly, leaving Mr Piggott nonplussed.

Mr Burbridge had descended from the carriage by the time she got there. Within seconds, Griffith joined them. Beth was appalled by the appearance of them both.

In the bright full light of day, her father's face was drawn and haggard. The doctor said his heart had been overstrained and that he needed rest. But this was more than that. Was he so worried about his debt to Mr Piggott that he had worn himself down to this state? Surely not—the carriage behind him was a testament to their status as being among the wealthiest families in the colony.

'Father,' said Griffith, 'I'll fetch you a seat.'

'What's this fussing about. Marriage has gelded you.' He gave a dry cackle. 'No chance of heirs that way, m'boy.'

Griffith's face, already grey, turned to granite.

'Papa,' Beth said urgently, 'don't you recall, dear Mary? We went to the funeral, Papa.'

Is Papa losing his mind?

'Yes, yes I remember. Next time, make sure you marry a breeder.'

'Papa.' Beth couldn't believe he was saying such things.

'Though why any woman would take you, I don't know. You've got a monkey on your back and it's never going to leave you alone.'

Griffith fell back, as if struck. 'I'll not stay for more of this, sir.' He took a few steps and then added, 'And you can go to hell, sir.'

Beth couldn't take it in. Papa shouldn't have said such things, but he must be losing his mind, if he had not already lost it. Surely Griffith could see that? She needed to find her mother. 'Griffith,' she called after him, following him back down the slope. 'He didn't mean it. He's not in his right mind. Ever since the robbery—'

'He didn't even lose so much as a penny, Beth.' He took a few more strides. 'Look, I went over to him because I thought he could do with a hand, and he shoves it back in my face. It's always the same.'

'He's a proud man, Griffith.'

'Well, pride is a luxury that he can't afford, as well he knows.'

'What do you mean?'

He ignored her. They'd reached the shore.

'I'm not sure Mother is going to be of much help,' he said. 'She looks completely worn out.'

'But she's the only one he'll listen to.'

They stepped across the rocks to where Mrs Burbridge was sitting with Rose, both staring out across to the racing boats. The wind was stronger now, and the sails scudded to and fro like the clouds above. The baron was no longer with them. Beth could see him back towards the trees, apparently giving an impromptu lecture to the Wood children on the properties of the plant lying limply in his hands.

'Mama,' Beth spoke gently as if to an invalid. 'We need a hand with Papa. He is not himself. Griffith and I—'

At this, Mrs Burbridge sat up straighter and turned to look at him. 'How are you faring?'

Griffith smiled gamely, obviously grateful for the balm of the enquiry. 'I'm holding up, Mother.'

Mrs Burbridge's piercing eyes narrowed. 'You don't look well. Have you been eating? Or are you reverting to old habits?'

'The Woods have been most kind and—'

'When all's said and done, you weren't married for long. Time heals all, as they say.' Mrs Burbridge turned back to the water. 'Mr Campbell's boat is quite the fastest, don't you think?'

Griffith, shaking his head in impotent fury, took the opportunity to leave.

Chapter 25

What is important in his life

Beth looked back to see where her father had got to. He was pacing up the roadway, away from the carriages. She and Rose would never get their mother to move quickly enough to catch up with him.

'You look exhausted, Mama,' Beth said hurriedly. 'Why don't Rose and I help you back under the trees. It's much more comfortable there. I'll bring Papa to join us. We'll all be able to watch the races together.'

Once they'd reach the trees, Mrs Burbridge allowed them to settle cushions on the ground for her, and Rose sat a little to the side. Beth hesitated, searching for any sight of Mr Burbridge.

'Sit, Beth, sit. It is quite tiring to see you fidgeting about. I am so exhausted, I can't think why,' Mrs Burbridge said. 'I confess that it has been taxing, taking care of him for the last while. Marriage isn't easy—not in the least.'

'I know, Mama,' Rose said, dourly.

'I don't think you do. Perhaps you can't, perhaps no one can before they marry. If you don't believe me, ask Henrietta—married that wastrel in a fit of—'

'Passion,' Rose blurted.

But her mother couldn't say the word. 'A fit of foolishness. Well, she rued the day, didn't she?'

'But you and Papa—' Rose began to protest.

'You know your father had been married before, didn't you?'

They didn't know. Beth stared at her mother, seeing the hardness behind her eyes.

'Died in childbirth, as so many women do,' her mother said with a hidden note of pride, as a woman who had borne and raised seven children. 'It left its mark, though.' She was silent for a while before she continued, 'When he decided to go back to England … We'd been here less than two years, and I couldn't see why he would go. But, well, you know your father.'

Beth looked to Rose to try to understand what their mother was telling them, but Rose was barely listening. She wasn't sure why her mother might think any of this was relevant to her. Or perhaps it had nothing to do with her at all, and her mother was so worn down that she couldn't help but confide her own travails.

'And then, when he came back after he'd been—' Mrs Burbridge's mouth tightened in anger. 'He'd wake in the night, sweating with fever, shouting and waking the household. He wouldn't let me out of his sight. He argued with everyone.' She'd been staring, unseeing. Suddenly, she looked at them. 'You wouldn't remember what he was like before, do you? You were too young.'

'I was two when he left for England,' Rose replied.

Beth's first memory of her father was soon after his return, four years later. She'd been allowed to join the adults after dinner in the drawing room. She'd been too frightened to approach him. She'd rushed into the drawing room, escaping the maid's guiding hands. Her father was still with Uncle Herbert, and the sound of their arguing voices carried across the hall. Four years in England had shrouded her father with a cloak of anger.

Bill and Griffith and their cousins had been playing cards but, to her delight, Henrietta had begun to play on the floor with her and her cousin, Charles. Beth remembered how Henrietta held out Bessie, her old rag doll, from the basket of toys. Charles had made a grab for Bessie, tugging the doll from Beth's grip. Bessie's arm ripped as Henrietta jerked the doll away from him, and Charles began yelling. Somehow it had all been connected to her father, but she didn't know why.

Beth realised that Mrs Burbridge was still talking, 'And now it's exactly like he was back then. And at that time, I thought that everything would return to how it had been. Things did improve, but, well—' She rubbed her fingers against her forehead, easing the creases. 'So, be sure about who you marry. You can't anticipate what life will bring, and you are bound together to share that life forever.'

Beth had heard versions of this homily before, but she had never understood what drove her mother to utter it.

'And so, who you marry needs to be your own decision—not mine, not your father's.'

For their mother to say such a thing felt blasphemous. Beth half-expected Reverend Marsden to waddle down the slope and smite them.

'It doesn't matter what we think about Baron von Hügel or Mr Justice Wood or even Mr Piggott for that matter; it doesn't matter whether we approve or disapprove. You will outlive us, as will your marriage.' Her voice was flat, her failure complete. Worn out by her brief flurry of conversation, she leaned back against the tree and soon fell into a doze.

'Do you know why Mama is talking about such things?' Beth asked quietly.

Rose glanced at her and then away again. 'I dare say you'll know soon enough. The baron is engaged.'

Beth waited.

'He was very polite, of course. "Your family have been most hospitable to me—you Rose, in particular," he said, "I would not wish it to be thought that I am unappreciative".'

Beth could see that these were words that Rose would never forget.

Rose went on. 'He said, "I had thought I might never wish to return to my homeland after the countess's marriage to Prince Metternich. I thought my happiness forever ruined".'

Beth held her breath.

'You know, for one moment, I dared to hope.' Rose shook her head. 'But no. He went on. "I am indeed fortunate to have found a woman who has made me the happiest of men". Apparently, it all happened before he arrived here. He was marooned by the monsoons in India, and a Colonel Farquharson managed to sort out all his arrangements. And the Colonel has a daughter.'

Beth found her voice. 'But why didn't he tell us before?'

'Apparently,' said Rose, and she closed her eyes, recalling his words, 'sometimes a man takes time to understand what is important in his life".' She shrugged ruefully.

It had been too long, and still her father had not reappeared. After the momentary distraction of the revelations about the baron, Beth's panic bubbled to the surface. Her mother still lay asleep, engulfed by the exhaustion of caring for her husband. Rose was lost in her own thoughts. It was as if they both had died and left Beth to carry on. Beth wanted to cry out like some child, railing against being told that it was time she grew up, time she let go of the comfort of knowing that there was always someone there to take action. Her steps were heavy as she trudged back up the slope again.

She stopped, out of breath. *But Henrietta, what about her?*

Henrietta, the eldest, the worldliest of them all, she should be the one looking after their mother, finding out what had shattered their father's mind. She scanned the picnicking group; she looked up to the rocky scrub at the height of the slope above; she swung back around, shielding her eyes against the sun, now full west and blinding.

There, in among the milling throng that had gone down to admire the winning sloop, was Henrietta. She was surrounded by laughing figures. She would get no help from Henrietta. The certainty dropped through her like lead shot.

Slowly, she resumed her climb—one step, then the next, looking as far as she needed to place her steps safely on the rough ground. Finally, she saw the wheels of the carriage in front of her. She checked inside. Empty.

The coil in her chest clutched at her heart and squeezed, and the world suddenly sped up. She strode further up the road where she had last seen her father. Perhaps he thought to walk back into town. She took a couple of steps in that direction. He wasn't the sort of person who walked. He wasn't well; he'd tire quickly.

He'd stop. He'd come back. He'd been restless, so he might continue pacing about.

She looked back the other way — low scrubby gorse and the rocky bones of sandstone, worn down by the winds. That way led to the east-facing cliff: a cliff so sheer that the picnicking parents on the harbour side slope below kept careful watch on their children lest they stray. It was a cliff that skylarking young men dared each other to approach, the crumbling edge waiting to take advantage of their foolhardiness. It was where, so the rumours whispered, the wretched found a way to end their misery.

'Miss Beth?' Mr Piggott panted. He'd followed her.

'I can't talk now. I have to find my father,' she gabbled.

'Your father can wait.' Mr Piggott took her by the shoulder. 'You both have kept me waiting long enough. I have been prepared to be patient. We are, after all, by way of being family, and —'

'I have to go, please, let me go.' Beth tried to wrench herself from his grip.

His hands tightened and she cried out with pain. He let go as suddenly as he had grabbed her. 'I'm sorry, I'm sorry.' He was shaking his head, tears in his eyes. 'I am not a violent man. I am not an impatient man. You must know this. But you and your father have me bound in chains. I need your answer, whatever it may be. I cannot move forward in my life until I know. You must see that, surely?'

Beth looked him directly in the eyes. As she did so, she realised that she had never looked him fully in the face before. His eyes were a warm hazel, shot through with flecks of gold. They were kind eyes. 'Then, I release you, Cousin Arthur,' she whispered. 'I cannot marry you.' She had never been as certain of anything in her life. She reached out her hand and touched him gently on his cheek.

His shoulders relaxed and he smiled. 'Thank you,' he whispered, taking her hand in his and kissing it lightly.

'I have to go,' she said, turning and then breaking into a run, lifting her skirts, each breath compressing her ribs against the prison of whalebone.

The closer she got to the cliff, the windier it got. Her bonnet flapped back, the ribbon around her neck strangling her. She tugged furiously at the ends and, released, the bonnet flew straight up, carried like an eagle on the updraught. All the time she ran, she searched for her father.

She found him sitting on the edge of the cliff, his legs dangling down over the side as if he were seated on a chair. His back was bowed, his head hanging, his forearms resting on his thighs, hands clasped.

Chapter 26

Your fall has a long life

Beth slowed to a walk. The wind was gusting so hard that her cheeks stung with the salt being blown up from the ocean below. She stopped at the last clump of pigface, too frightened to tread on the loose sandy soil. 'Papa?'

He didn't move.

'Papa?' Louder now, to be heard above the wind.

He flinched but didn't turn.

'Come back from the edge, please Papa. You're frightening me.'

'Get back,' he shouted, whether to prevent her stopping him or wary for her safety, she didn't know.

She knew she didn't have the strength to pull him back, even if she dared to approach closer.

His shoulders were shaking.

She took a step away from the safety of the tussock. Then she took another and she was close enough to see over the edge. It was a straight drop to the rocks below. She staggered as a blast of wind shoved her off balance.

'Get back, I said.' Her father twisted around, one hand flung out as if to save her.

'Come with me.' Beth grasped his hand. If he tried to shake her off then she'd fall, she knew it. The sound of the ocean thrashing the rocks drowned the shrieking wind roaring up the cliff face. 'I won't let go.'

His cheeks were raw with tears and spray. But his grip was firm. She could feel the warmth. His touch was entirely foreign to her, yet so familiar, as if recalled from long ago. It was as if she were being held: a baby cradled in her father's hands.

'Come back,' she said again, too soft to be heard.

Yet, come he did.

He swung one leg back and twisted so that he knelt before her. She watched his white hair ruffle back with the wind, exposing the pink of his scalp—so vulnerable, so pitiable. With her help, he stumbled back to an outcrop of sandstone among the scrubby bushes. With the sudden diminution of the noise of the cliff, it felt like her ears were stoppered with wool. But when he spoke, quietly and brokenly, she could hear every word.

'We're ruined, Beth, ruined. When Piggott sues for his repayment, then there will be nothing for it but to sell up. With the market the way it is now, we won't even get enough to pay him, let alone all the other creditors.'

Beth realised now the significance of her brother Bill's furrowed brow and Griffith's comments. But her father was a great businessman, everyone said so. He was the one who gave advice, and people had themselves to blame if they disregarded it, or so he had always said. Beth closed her eyes. The core of the family's fortunes was rotted away with debt, while to their outside appearance there was only pinprick evidence that a fruit fly had bored into the flesh.

'If he'd come but a few years ago, then we'd have been able to repay him twice over. But he had to dilly-dally, didn't he? Had to delay until his own firm went to the devil, and then the fool imagines that, because we're here on the other side of the world, that the same forces haven't threatened us all.' He shook his head. 'I've told him. Wait, I said. Never sell when the market is low. If we wait, then it'll be better for us both. Just wait.' He shook his head. 'Says he can't afford to wait. Says he has nought to live on without it. I doubt that. But with Giles Wood on his side.' Her father's voice dripped with hatred. 'He's feeling bold, and he'll push and push, and then—'

Her father laid all the blame for his impending ruin on Mr Piggott and Mr Wood. He'd said nothing about the solution of marriage. Beth felt the shame of her refusal. If she'd agreed to marry Mr Piggott, then he would have waited, like her father had said. Perhaps if she found Mr Piggott and said she'd changed her mind?

'But we'll manage, Papa,' she sought to reassure him. 'You are greatly respected, and people will understand our situation. We'll make do somehow, even if our circumstances are substantially reduced.'

'You are as innocent as I was once.' He smiled sourly. 'I suppose I can't expect you to benefit from my experience if I have striven to keep it from you.' He was staring back out over the ocean.

Beth feared he might suddenly make a run for the cliff and throw himself off the edge. She placed her hand softly over his.

'Your mother and I don't talk about it much, although of course it's a matter of record and those who were here at the time know all about it. They tend not to bring it up to my face, particularly now that I've reached the position of being close to the governor's ear.' His voice cracked at little at the mention of his recent appointment to the Legislative Council. That too would be lost.

'What?' Beth's imagination couldn't stretch that far.

'Not long after you'd been born,' he began, 'I ran afoul of the governor of the time. You've heard of Bligh, I daresay.' He didn't wait for an answer. 'Thought he could run the place like a naval prison camp and make a bit for himself on the side while he was at it. No recognition that there were free men in the place. No vision of the future. As far as he was concerned, any business that was conducted in the colony was for the benefit of the British government, as embodied by him, of course. Well, a few of the free settlers—'

'Mr Macarthur,' interrupted Beth, remembering fragments of overhead gossip. The history of the colony, short as it was, had not warranted supplanting their lessons about the Kings and Queens of England.

'And many others, including me and your Uncle Herbert. Well, it was a pathetic scuffle in the end, but we did manage to send Bligh packing, though he skulked in his ship in the harbour like a bad smell until he decided to head down to Van Diemen's Land and get Lieutenant-Governor Collins to help him sort things out. We all knew that wasn't going to work, Collins being a man with some sense, so we figured that Bligh would hightail it back to England, and once there, he could spread as many lies as he liked. Well, we held a public meeting and the upshot was that Macarthur, seeing as he was a man with the right connections back home, should set sail immediately so as to get there before him and put the matter on record. Well, you know what I think of Macarthur.'

Beth had endured endless diatribes about the many character faults of one of their closer neighbours. But it was only as he went on that she began to understand.

'So, what did Macarthur do? Sat about, glorying in what he would say and to whom, and on and on, but still he didn't go. He waited so long that he was still here when Paterson finally saw fit to take over the reins, sending Major Johnston off to England to face court martial. So Herbert and I knew that one of us should go and appear as a witness, and it was decided that I should go.' His face darkened. 'All good fortune to my brother,' he added bitterly. 'I went. At the Cape of Good Hope, I was arrested on Bligh's instructions to the governor, Lord Caledon.'

Beth stared. She heard the words, but it was as if they were in another language. Never could she have imagined those words being uttered by her father.

He drew a deep breath. 'I was stripped, rough-handled into a cell. It was filthy, crawling with vermin. Jail fever was the least of the illnesses I could have caught. My fever brought me delusions, and one minute I was back here—sailing into the harbour for the first time again, the clanking of the anchor chains mooring us in our new land—and then the noise turned into a nightmare of chains being fastened to my ankles and wrists, and then—' He broke off. He was shaking as if fever had once more engulfed him, just as he had done after facing down the robbers.

That day seemed forever ago, when the father she had known had disappeared.

'People rejoice in your downfall, Beth,' he said after a while. 'And your fall has a long life.'

Tiredness engulfed her. She'd helped get him back from the cliff, but there was nothing she could do to help him against memories such as these. They sat together without speaking until the sound of cannon fire from Dawes Point boomed across the harbour waters behind them, signalling the end of the boat races.

'I don't suppose you had a bet on a winner?' she asked as she helped him stand.

He gave her a half-smile. 'You?' he asked.

No, she thought, but she did know that she needed to have a word with Cousin Arthur.

Chapter 27

Mr Piggott, may I have a word

The walk back to the carriage with her father was a long one. Her father was reduced to shuffling along, stopping every few feet to lean heavily on her shoulder. His colour was high, and she could feel the heat of his fever radiating from him. He shouldn't have come out today; he was too unwell.

Beth wondered how her mother could have ever thought he was up to an excursion as extended as this one. If he'd stayed at home, though, her mother would have had to stay with him. Perhaps she'd thought to gain a brief respite by bringing him along where there were so many others to assist. She could feel her father's anguish but, paradoxically, knowing that he was depending on her in his suffering brought with it a kind of joy of its own. She would do more if she could.

The picnickers had taken the cannon fire to mean the end of the day. The roadway lined with carriages was churning with lost children and their vexed parents, past whom servants tried to navigate, some laden with empty picnic baskets and others with bundles of cushions and blankets perched on their heads. Through all of this, the niceties of farewells and arrangements for next meetings must be observed.

As slow as Beth and Mr Burbridge were, they were the first in the family to make their way through the crowds and reach the carriages. She helped her father climb in, and he slumped back exhausted into the corner, closing his eyes, breathing heavily. She stood with her back to the carriage, searching for Mr Piggott.

She moved through the throng until she met Rose helping Mrs Burbridge up the slope.

'Miss Burbridge?'

It was Mr Justice Wood. He looked intensely at Rose while he gently disengaged his hand from which his youngest was clinging and gave her over to the charge of their governess.

Rose grasped Beth's hand to prevent her from leaving.

'If I might speak with you a moment?' The loss of Mary had traced another layer of grief through the dark rings under his eyes. On his lips played the promise of a smile; a smile reserved for Rose's answer, perhaps.

'I had hoped to spend some time with you earlier,' he began.

'Ah, Miss Burbridge,' came the voice of Baron von Hügel as he strode towards them, his manner all jollity.

Mr Justice Wood took a step back, his eyes tracking between Rose and the baron.

Beth smiled nervously at Mr Wood. 'I was glad you and your family were all able to come to the regatta, and especially that you were able to convince Griffith to accompany you. It would not do for him to be left alone in his melancholy.'

Mr Wood kept his eyes on Rose and the baron. 'Yes, Griffith seems to enjoy the company of my own children nearly as much as he does Mrs Richeley's.'

'He enjoys making mischief with them, I think you mean,' Beth replied, trying to keep him occupied.

'Mrs Burbridge is most fortunate to have such attentive daughters,' the baron was saying to Rose.

He means 'spinster daughters', Beth thought: *daughters who remain by their parents' side until the end.*

The baron had taken a few steps when, apparently struck by a thought, he said, 'We are in such a rush to get the collection ready for the journey, I wonder, Miss Burbridge, would you perhaps enjoy working with us to assist? Your expertise would be most appreciated.'

There was a moment, a mere second, but an abyss in time, where all four of them waited—Rose's eyes on the baron, Mr Wood watching Rose, and Beth transfixed.

'Of course,' replied Rose. 'I have some thought to undertake a journey myself—to Kent. If you like, I could undertake to transport those seed pods we discussed?'

She said it so effortlessly, with such quiet confidence, that Beth realised that this was no whim, no casual aside, but a long-held plan to pursue her devotion.

'If I do not see you before you depart,' Mr Justice Wood addressed the baron formally, 'I wish you good speed.' He bowed slightly to Rose. 'And to you also, Miss Burbridge, wherever your travels might take you.'

Their little tableau disintegrated.

Mrs Burbridge, who had been drawn aside by Mr and Mrs McPhail in passing, returned.

'Did I hear correctly, Rose? You think to pursue this matter?'

'The baron has paid me the highest compliment by asking me for assistance. I mean to help him, Mama. His wife will have many duties. But even if I can only contribute in some small way to his botanical pursuits, then so be it. It will be enough.'

Mrs Burbridge frowned and shook off Rose's proffered arm as they moved onward.

Beth, freed from the tight clasp of Rose's hand, searched the crowd. Mr Piggott, who previously had haunted her every move, had disappeared.

'Have you seen Mr Piggott?'

'Now that's not a question I thought to hear from you,' Henrietta replied. 'I rather got the impression you were avoiding our dear cousin.'

Beth had found Henrietta still lingering near the water's edge. The shadows of the dying afternoon scoured the faint lines across her face. She was getting older. They all were.

'All these sails,' mused Henrietta. 'They make me reminisce.' She added, 'Do you think I would have made a bad wife for a sailor?'

'I, I didn't … I mean, I have no thoughts as to that,' Beth stammered, caught off guard.

'Perhaps I would have.'

'I know I should not have interfered.'

'No.' Henrietta paused. 'But then, perhaps it was all a dream. It felt like it might be at the time. I didn't really believe it myself. I have tried to forget about it.' She put her arm through Beth's and they began the walk to the carriages.

'Baron de Bougainville was exceedingly handsome.' Beth smiled.

Henrietta smiled back. 'He was indeed. And he was in love with me. So very sad for him, don't you think?'

'What, have you broken some other poor chap's heart?' Griffith said. 'I've come to tell you two to get a hurry on. If you don't collect your children soon, then Eliza is going to completely turn little Susannah's head with tales of her mother's life in India. She has you charming Maharajahs and riding elephants and —'

'All true, all true.' Henrietta laughed. 'But don't tell me that I've passed down Mama's tale-telling to my own dear child?'

'Tell me, Beth,' asked Griffith. 'Has the day been wasted? Or has Rose managed to find herself a husband? Mr Wood or some baron or other. My sister here assures me that barons are the best candidates for romance.'

Henrietta gave him a jab with her elbow.

'No,' Beth answered. 'No to both, is the answer.'

'I'm disappointed,' Henrietta said. 'Barons are not worth the time and trouble, of course.' She gave Beth a quick smile. 'But Mr Justice Wood is a most agreeable gentleman, don't you think?'

'Indeed,' said Griffith.

'No, I mean it. He is wise and respected by all—'

'Except Papa.'

'Well, yes, exactly.'

'But how far do we value our father's opinion?' Griffith added in agreement.

Henrietta went on. 'And, let me see, Giles Wood is witty, intelligent, kind, loves his children, and should I continue?'

When they reached the carriage, Henrietta's daughter raced up to join them.

'Do you need a hand, sir?' Griffith smiled as Mr Justice Wood approached, surrounded by the other children.

'Yours, I think, Mrs Richeley,' Mr Wood said, indicating Alec and Artie.

'I hope they haven't been leading your children into too much mischief,' Henrietta said, frowning in mock sternness at the two lads. Their faces glowed with the effects of the sun, wind and exercise of the day.

'Not at all,' Mr Wood replied. 'Or, at least, no more mischief than I would expect from children of such a spirited mother, if you don't mind me saying.' His smile was warmly appreciative. 'Now, come along the rest of you.'

There were groans all round as the children affected reluctance.

'I'm glad you're here, Henrietta,' Griffith said suddenly. 'I don't think I could do this without you.'

She squeezed his hand.

'And, you know,' he said, resuming his usual banter, 'I'm beginning to think that I detect a glint of something brewing between you and Giles Wood. Better watch yourself, old girl, you'll end up a judge's wife, and who knows where that might lead.'

'Did Beth and I ever tell you about poor Mrs Wood's dying wish ...? Henrietta began.

Seeing Mr Piggott at last, Beth left the rest of the story to Henrietta and slipped away. She walked swiftly, dodging people, a trout fighting its way upstream, until she reached him. 'Mr Piggott, may I have a word.' She wasn't asking.

He stopped, uncertain.

'It has occurred to me, Mr Piggott, that there is something you have failed to tell your mentor, Mr Justice Wood, the man who has been so kind as to support your claim upon my father. Something that might change his position if he were to know it.'

He frowned, doubt showing in his eyes.

'As I understand it, you have argued against my father's suggestion that you hold off from reclaiming the debt until the financial markets improve, as improve they must, indeed as they always do, given time. Mr Wood has tried enough cases of bankruptcy to be aware that selling on a falling market is an imprudent course of action, warranted only in extreme circumstances. I think you have given him to believe that your circumstances are extreme, in that you find yourself without means of support without payment of the debt.'

Mr Piggott tried to speak.

Beth went on regardless. 'Yet, you yourself told me that Palmer and Company have offered you a position with their firm. They have even given you the choice of their offices in London or Canton, as best suits. What might Mr Justice Wood recommend in his wisdom, were he to be apprised of this information?'

His fingers plucked nervously at his buttons.

'I suggest, Mr Piggott, that you might find your best course of action is to advise Mr Justice Wood that, due to this unexpected change in your circumstances, you consider that your most prudent course of action is to cease pursuing us for the recovery of the debt, in the full confidence that my father will pay back the monies owed at a later time—to the mutual advantage of you both.'

He nodded mutely, too shaken to speak.

Beth left him there and strode effortlessly back up the last part of the slope to the carriage. She felt her chest expand and her shoulders release as if she had let fall a heavy weight. 'Mama, here let me help,' she said as her mother baulked at the carriage steps.

Rose was already in the carriage, staring out the window, apparently oblivious of their mother's need.

Beth, with a gentle pressure at her mother's back and her other arm under her elbow, guided her mother up the steps and into the carriage. She settled her on the seat, tucking a light rug around her knees. 'We'll all be home in no time at all,' she murmured as she took her place opposite Rose.

'Always such a help, dearest Beth,' said her mother, leaning her head back with a sigh.

Rose caught Beth's eye and nodded her approval.

THE END

244

One of the greatest areas of difficulty in writing this novel was in reconciling the views of the historical characters about race and class with contemporary cultural awareness.

In the early 1800s, the era in which the novel is set, Sydney was a small settlement of about 30,000 people, about two-thirds of whom were convicts or ex-convicts, with the convict population almost at its peak. The population was rapidly growing, so social connections were continually changing and adjusting. The historical characters of this novel lived among a small elite (the 'exclusives') within a penal colony, where the main source of labour for their homes and estates was provided by convicts, convicts' children, and convicts who had served their time ('emancipists'). The emancipists thrived on the business opportunities in the new colony, with many becoming as rich or richer than their former masters. The class sensibilities of the free elite therefore were necessarily pragmatically blind where business was concerned, though it was still acute in social situations.

The settlement sat at the edge of a large continent populated by multiple Aboriginal tribes whose clan groups were being progressively dispossessed with the uptake of land as the colony grew. The contact between

European settlers and Indigenous peoples was at its most direct and most conflicted in areas of new occupation, for example, in the Hunter region. The attitudes described in this novel were based on family records and were typical of the landed class. I have tried to capture something of this selective blindness through contrasting the perspectives of the historical figures of Baron de Bougainville and Baron von Hügel, who as visitors to the colony recorded very strong impressions about the European and Indigenous inhabitants in their journals.

I have drawn heavily from available historical records to paint a picture of the lives of the main characters in this novel. I have fictionalised the names of the main characters because I cannot know their personal feelings and motivations, and so the novel's plot, events and themes are my own invention. Thus, the Burbridge and Wood families and their relatives by birth or marriage are fictional characters. However, I have retained the names of well-known historical figures who appear or who are referred to in the novel, and for whom considerable material is available upon which to ground their depiction.

For a longer factual account of the events and people who inspired this work of fiction, readers may be interested in the short biography I have written previously on the life of Harriet Blaxland.

A Ferguson, *A gentleman's daughter: The life of Harriet Mary Dowling (nee Blaxland) in India and Australia in colonial times*, Backstory Press, New South Wales, 2017.

(available in e-book or paperback via Amazon)

Acknowledgements

Once again my husband, Ian King, gets top billing in my list of 'thankyou's. Without his detailed background knowledge of the Blaxland history and his constant support and encouragement, this project would have stalled a long time ago. My thanks are also owed to Richard Blaxland and Wendy Blaxland for their enthusiastic support. I am very appreciative of the librarians at the State Library of New South Wales for enabling my access to their collection which includes materials related to the Blaxland, Dowling and Walker families.

My thanks to the members of the Lake Macquarie branch of the Fellowship of Australian Writing for their support and invaluable feedback in the development of this novel and my other writing over many years. Thanks also to my trusty beta-readers—Jenny Ferneyhough, Sue McAllister, and Glenys Murray—for their insightful comments and suggestions on this story and all the others. And finally, thanks too for the polish to the final product from the detailed editing provided courtesy of the Manuscript Appraisal Agency, Katoomba, New South Wales. Any remaining glitches remain, of course, my own.

About the author

After completing a degree in writing in the early 70s, my interest in communication led me to qualify and work as a speech pathologist in clinical and academic settings. Now retired, I am pursuing my long-standing fascination with story writing across diverse genres.

In 2017, I self-published 'A Gentleman's Daughter'—a biography of Harriet Blaxland (later, Lady Dowling) who lived a colourful life in colonial New South Wales and India (available in paperback and eBook through Amazon and other online retailers). Over the last few years, I have written a number of award-winning short stories ranging across crime, horror, and historical science fiction. My unpublished science-fiction novel 'Grey Nomad' was shortlisted for the 2019 Fantastic Prize (Brio Books), the Queensland Writers' Centre 2020 Adaptable and Publishable programs, and I currently have a crime novel 'in the works'.

Next in the trilogy

Volume 3

in The Sisters' Saga

Widow's Wake is the last of three in *The Sisters' Saga*, which tells of three sisters and the compromises they must make to reconcile love's delusions with the demands of reality.

In this short historical fiction novel, over the course of a single voyage from Sydney to London in 1847, Henrietta must reconcile the regrets of her past in order to truly cast aside her widow's weeds and embrace the adventures ahead.

She is the heroine of the colourful tales she shares with young Mr Morgan Mayhew. However, their 1847 voyage from Sydney to London will be one tale neither will ever divulge.